غريب

WARRIORS & WARLOCKS

Chapter One: Outcast

منذر القباني

Monther AlKabbani

@MontherKabbani

Translated by Timothy Gregory

Monther AlKabbani

منذر القباني

The League of Arabic SciFiers

AlKabbani ،Monther

    Warriors and Warlocks. / AlKabbani ،Monther .- Jeddah ,
    2019

    290p ;

    1- Stories   I-Title

    813.039531 dc   1440/ 10588

    L.D. no.   1440/ 10588

    ISBN-13:   978-603-03-1279-5

Sales@Yatakhayaloon.com

The League of Arabic SciFiers

Yatakhayaloon: The League of Arabic SciFiers, was founded to establish the Arabian Science Fiction Genre, making it stand out as a unique and new view of Sci-Fi that would also expose the world to our rich Arabian culture.

www.Yatakhayaloon.com
www.يتخيلون.com

info@yatakhayaloon.com
@Yatakhayaloon

3

All praise be to the Creator who made this world for the righteous

And for every seeker; it was He who made the phenomena and secrets

---

Prologue

It would be the very definition of the word insanity to try to rescue Borte from the clutches of the Merkit. What could he and his handful of horsemen possibly do against a thousand men? Only a lunatic would try to retrieve his wife after Chiledu, the Merkit's Khan, had kidnapped her. There was no tribe Temujin could call on to join him on a raid. He was just an outcast, a wanderer, sheltered by a few who held to their friendship to Yesugei Khan, Temujin's father. Temujin wasn't even ten years old when the Tatars poisoned Yesugei. The tribe broke up after that, but the khan's son remained an outcast; the boy and his mother deserted by his father's supporters. All but his betrothed. She never gave up on him, it was she who insisted that her father honor the marriage contract he had made with Yesugei. The girl knew that Temujin would not be an outcast forever. She believed that the young Mongol, who held the keys to her heart, would one day conquer all his enemies. "It is the will of Tengri, Lord of the Blue Sky, so speak the spirits. This boy is destined to stand above all. He shall accomplish what no other has before him and none shall after him. He will weave the impossible from the threads of despair and the world shall bend beneath his feet."

Tabtinkar, the shaman, told Yesugei Khan when his wife gave birth to a son, born holding a clot of blood in his right hand.

Many of the steppes' residents had heard of Tabtinkar's prophecy, but few believed. Borte was one of those few, as were the seven warriors on horseback who accompanied Temujin as he went to retrieve his wife from the Merkit's clutches.

***

On that moonless night, silence fell over the Merkit camp after their celebration. One raid after another had confirmed Chiledu's place as one of the strongest khans on the steppes. No khan from any neighboring tribe had the strength to stand against his horsemen. Instead, they tried to curry favor by offering him a plethora of gifts including horses and mountains of wool and grain. Some had declared themselves his subjects, obedient to his command. Others simply felt that giving him their goods was a better alternative than forfeiting their lives and the lives of their families. Their actions led Chiledu to believe that no one living within his range on the steppes had the wherewithal to stand up to him. And here, surrounded by his warriors … only a fool would believe he could penetrate the Merkit camp, and Chiledu feared no fool. Fools were never the victors; they were always the vanquished.

***

Temujin kept his distance, waiting in the brush as he watched the camp. His seven horsemen kept their eyes on him, watching in silence, waiting for him to reveal his plan to rescue Borte. They had absolute faith in his leadership and would follow without question. They knew that Temujin would never make a move on a mission like this without having a well-formed plan for infiltrating the Merkit camp unseen. Maybe he had a spy among the Merkit and was waiting for a signal indicating all the horsemen were asleep. Or he might ask his men to split up around the outskirts of the camp to cause a diversion, keeping the Merkit occupied as he went alone to the tent where Borte was being held to rescue her. In any case, they were ready to die for him this night. They each had their own story with Temujin, and every story ended with an oath of absolute fealty and a vow to lay down their lives for him. Not one of them even considered breaking his vow tonight.

But Temujin would not ask them to disperse around the camp or to infiltrate it under the cover of darkness. Instead, he asked them to remain hidden where they were as he advanced on the Merkit alone. He ordered them to stay where they were until Borte arrived. When she did, they were to take her back to their own camp immediately, without a backward glance. He made them swear before Tengri that they would leave the instant Borte came and that they would not wait for him. They tried to talk him out of it. They offered many alternative plans, none of which included his going into the Merkit camp alone. It was to no avail, however. The way things were, he had to go without his men—Temujin planned to bring more than just Borte back with him!

***

Entering his tent, pitched in the center of the Merkit camp, surrounded by the tents of more than a thousand horsemen, Chiledu did not know what surprise awaited in his pallet, no khan on the Asian steppes would have anticipated it. Generations of khans from every tribe had learned that the strong rule the weak, that the strong can take valuables and women as spoils from the weak, along with anything else they wanted. The life of a horse warrior of the steppes resembled the lives of wolves. There were the strong and there were the weak. There were those who conquered and those who were vanquished. It was the duty of the defeated to tuck their tails between their legs and run home, bearing with them the shame their weakness brought upon their tribes. So it was that when Chiledu came upon Borte that evening, after celebrating with his men over mugs of fermented mare's milk, he was looking forward to taking his pleasure from her. He was filled with lust in a way that he had never felt for any other woman. Who had not heard of Borte's legendary beauty, her agility of mind, and her courage? *A woman like that only comes once in a generation. That bumbling boy Temujin does not deserve a woman like her!*

Borte was laying on the low pallet, covered by a piece of hide. Chiledu moved to her, dropping down on top of her. With his right hand wrapped in the hair at the back of her head, he stripped her with his left. Borte did not resist. She remained still and silent, knowing that there was no point to fighting with a man like Chiledu who was so much stronger than she. Instead, she waited for just the right opportunity. She waited for the moment when he would be lost in his passion, in the throes of his ejaculation. She waited as his breath quickened in pace with the lurching thrusts of his fat thighs. Over and over again until she finally felt the weight of his body fall away from her back. When she twisted to look, she found him stretched out next to her, his eyes closed. This was her moment!

Without the slightest hesitation, Borte pulled Chiledu's dagger from the sheath at his belt and, using every ounce of strength in her body, before the Merkit Khan sensed anything, she slit his throat and then plunged the dagger between his thighs. That was where she left the blade, a sign to any who may yet harbor thoughts of kidnapping her.

Temujin approached the Merkit camp. Nocking two arrows to his bowstring, he released one then the other, taking down two of the Merkit warriors guarding the eastern entrance to the camp. The third had only just noticed what had happened to his fellows when an arrow pierced his throat and he went down. Under cover of the starless night, Temujin continued towards the Merkit camp, aiming for the place where Chiledu was bedded down. Exiting his tent to relieve himself, a fourth warrior stumbled upon Temujin, but before he was even aware of a stranger in the camp, Temujin's sword had passed through his neck, dropping the man's corpse to the dry ground that thirsted for the rain gathering in the clouds above. Temujin arrived at his goal with little trouble. When he opened the tent, he found Borte rushing towards him as though she had known he was coming.

"My heart told me you would come tonight." She said, taking his round face in her hands and rubbing the side of her nose to his.

"Forgive me," Temujin said, dropping to his knees before her. "I should never have lost you."

Borte took his arm, tugging him back to his feet. "But you came for me. You did not give up on me. That's what matters."

Temujin took Borte's wrist and walked her to the back of the tent. With his dagger, he slit open a back door just large enough for her slight form to fit through.

"My men are waiting for you to the east of the camp. Hurry. Go to them now before the Merkit notice what's happened."

"What about you? Aren't you coming with me?" She asked.

Temujin looked at Chiledu's corpse on the ground in the middle of the tent. "It's time for a new khan to rise. You go now. I will soon return at the head of nine hundred Merkit warriors. I promise."

"Nine hundred?" She asked, "Don't you mean a thousand?"

"No… Just nine hundred. I'll have to kill a hundred of them before the rest will serve me."

***

Temujin left the tent, approaching a dark horse nearby. The horse started at his approach but calmed quickly enough as Temujin placed his right hand on its shoulder and whispered in its ear before jumping on its back. It was only a few moments before one of the warriors raised the alarm when he discovered Chiledu's body. In moments the Merkit horsemen had found and surrounded Temujin, some of the men had nocked arrows and taken aim, ready to loose and take their revenge in blood, believing that he had murdered their Khan. For some reason none dared approach him; they simply surrounded him. The standoff continued until Chamukei, Chiledu's eldest son, appeared. He went straight for Temujin, his towering rage clearly visible on his face.

"How does a rat like you dare to kill his betters? By the Lord of the Sky, I will tear you limb from limb – you and your entire tribe, then I will feed your remains to the wolves of the steppes!"

Chamukei drew his sword from its sheath, but at that instant, the sky chose to let loose a flood of rain pouring from the clouds above. There was a blinding flash of lightning followed by deafening thunder and accompanied by a sudden chill as hailstones pounded down from the heavens as if launched by catapults.

When Chamukei could see again, the dark horse was no longer where it had been. He spun to his right then to the left, casting about for Temujin, shouting at the warriors around him, ordering them to find him and bring him back alive. His search was brief. Temujin's sword appeared out of nowhere and separated Chamukei's head from his shoulders. As the body fell, a barrage of arrows flew towards the remaining Merkit, felling one after another until nearly a hundred were dead.

***

Tabtinkar the shaman emerged from his tent, ending the self-imposed seclusion he had started when Temujin left to rescue Borte. She had returned to the camp two days earlier. When he got to the top of a hill to the west of the camp established up by the seven warriors, he stopped to watch the sun. Borte was sitting on the same hilltop, watching the horizon, hoping to catch a glimpse of Temujin.

"He told me he would come, leading the Merkit horsemen. If only I hadn't left him! I should have stayed." Borte's voice carried her anxiety, concern, and fear.

"Temujin will return, but the Merkit will not be the only warriors following him. He will lead an army that unifies Turk, Niman, Merkit, Tatar, and Croat. All of them shall fight under the Mongol banner. Even Kurds, Arabs, and Chinese will find places for themselves in his army. The time has come, Borte." He told her. "It is time. Do you see this sky? The sky has one master, just one owner. The earth is no different. There shall be a single khan who dominates all. A great khan who stands above the khans, kings, and sultans of this earth. A universal Khan -- Genghis Khan."

"Oh, greatest of shamans, if that is so, why do I read worry in your expression?"

Tabtinkar stood silent for a time, continuing his examination of the sunset before he replied. "I do not worry about what shall be, Borte. I worry about what random chance."

"Random chance?" she asked, "Is fate not set in stone?"

"That" he replied, "is what worries me."

"What could happen?"

"I saw a fierce dog separate itself from a pack of wolves. He drove them all out, then ascended to heaven."

Borte's closed her eyes when she heard what Tabtinkar had seen and was filled with terror. She knew very well what it meant. She knew that if what he said came to pass, the consequences would be dire.

"When do you think this may happen?"

The shaman turned and met the eyes of his Khan's wife and answered, "With the passing of Spring."

(1)
A World without Spring

"The Egyptian presidential elections ended with the anticipated victory of Mr. Gamal Mubarak, with 85% of the votes. This marks the first time that Egypt will be under a civilian president in the nearly sixty years since the July Revolution.

"In other news, Mrs. Layla Al-Tarabalsi, President of Tunisia, announced her nation's intent to host the Arab League Conference."

Murad turned off his car radio. The headache that had bothered him that morning had come back with a vengeance. Something told him the headache was unrelated to his fast for Ramadan, which had been his theory up to that point. Instead, he sensed it might be tied to the dream he had been having for twenty years. *How can a dream repeat again and again like that for such a long period of time?* The whole thing was strange. Maybe it was stress, born from his concern over the turmoil in his life this past year that precipitated his move from Jeddah to Riyadh. If the content of this recurring dream was not connected to the events that brought him to Riyadh, events that still caused heartache and a lump in his throat, well...

***

Life is very strange. Nothing stays the same. A person's entire world can be tossed upside-down between one sunset and the next. The world you know when you go to bed at night could be unrecognizable to the one you had found upon waking that morning. That was how it went for Murad Qutuz when he came to the Jeddah University Hospital early that morning nearly a year ago. That same recurring dream had awakened him that morning, and the headache came with it. He didn't know then that, even as he stepped into the surgery wing of the hospital to check on his patient, the one who had reconstructive surgery following breast cancer treatment, he had laid the foundation for a series of events that would change the course of his life forever. Those events and their consequences left him full of questions: "What if... What if I had arrived at the hospital later? What if Hadeel hadn't seen me on the wing when I went to visit the patient? What if the patient hadn't been Hadeel's sister? What if Hadeel weren't a doctor at my hospital? What if I had not met her at all? We couldn't have fallen for each other..." It seemed like he would never run out of these questions. They filled his mind to the point of exhaustion, and they started on the day he signed his letter of resignation – a resignation forced on him in order to avoid a scandal.

***

Hadeel followed him to his office that day when he finished his rounds. She needed to tell him that her father had not approved of his proposal to marry her.

16

Murad's assistant professorship, teaching surgery at the faculty of medicine, didn't help his case with her father. Neither did his status as one of the best cosmetic surgeons, nor continuing his work as a serious academic, dedicated to research, teaching students, and mentoring doctors in training. He had achieved all this before he hit 35. Hadeel's feelings for him, her desire to marry him and no one else, didn't help, either. None of this mattered to her father. Her well-to-do family, proud of its pure Arabian blood, would never allow her to marry an Abkhazian man who would give her children with slanted eyes and squashed noses. Even Wajih, married to the sister that Murad had operated on, stood strongly opposed to their marriage. "To be my wife's doctor is one thing, but to be my brother-in-law is something else entirely!" The genes of Central Asia had no place in Hadeel's pure-blooded Arab family.

Murad Qutuz knew the family's answer just by looking at Hadeel's face. He didn't need her to say a word, the eloquence of her eyes needed no validation from her voice.

"What are you doing at the hospital so early? I still have two hours left on my shift." He asked, though he knew exactly why she had come early. She wanted to talk to him in person, and before the place filled up with doctors, students, and administrative staff.

Hadeel sat in the chair across from him without answering his question, her eyes shifting from him to the floor and back again. The silence stretched out for a time as she mustered her strength and courage to speak:

"Murad…"

The instant his name left her lips, a man barged in on them with a harried look.

"Wajih! What are you doing here? Is Hana alright?"

"Your sister told me that the doctor had been by to see her. She also said she had seen you in the hall. I'm glad I decided to stop by the hospital on my way to the airport so I could see this farce for myself!"

Murad knew why this man looked agitated, and it had nothing to do with his wife's health.

"What gives you the right to talk to me like that?" She asked, "You aren't my guardian! And don't forget, this is where I work, and that Dr. Murad is my colleague."

"No, Hadeel. You know perfectly well that he is more than just a colleague!"

At that moment, Murad decided that he had to intervene to try and keep things from getting more out of hand than they already were, with both of them starting to shout.

"Guys, it isn't worth all this. It's just a misunderstanding."

"Shut up, you! It's none of your business!"

"Wajih!"

Wajih stormed out, his few words were enough – like bullets from a sniper rifle aiming to kill. As if being denied and hearing from Wajih weren't enough, the situation continued to escalate as the day wore on.

***

The department chair summoned him to come at once. Then came the summons from the dean of the College of Medicine. The next day, the summons came from the university's administrator.

Murad knew that there had been a complaint filed against him. The department chair didn't tell him in so many words, and neither did the dean. Each of them left it at telling him that the situation was extremely serious, enough so that the university administrator got involved.

"I'm sorry we can't say more than that. It's for the best for you to take a leave of absence until the whole thing blows over." No matter how he pried, neither the department head nor the dean would say more. The next morning, however, when he met with the university administrator, it was a different story.

"You must know, doctor, this is very serious. That's why I wanted to talk to you personally and without delay. This isn't just about your reputation; it impacts the reputation of the whole university."

The administrator's words hit Murad like a bolt from the blue, particularly since he had no idea what the administrator was talking about. Shock and incomprehension were clearly readable on his face.

"The husband of one of your patients filed a complaint against you. If it weren't for the prestigious social standing of the person filing the complaint, and the gravity of the charge, we would normally let the issue run its natural course through an investigation. But, fortunately, I have a good relationship with Mr. Wajih."

"Wajih!" he interjected, now getting an inkling of what the administrator was talking about. "There is some kind of misunderstanding. Dr. Hadeel came to see me in order to check on her sister. You know she is in my department, and she is well regarded. But her brother-in-law got the wrong idea."

"Dr. Hadeel came to you to check on her sister? Or was it to confront you about what you did?" The question seemed to come out of nowhere, setting Murad back on his heels.

"What do you mean?"

"You have been accused of molesting Mr. Wajih's wife, in retaliation for the family's refusal to allow you to marry her sister, Dr. Hadeel."

Each time he recalled these events, a blur lasting less than 48 hours, his desire to wipe this brief period of absurdity from his life intensified. But something within, for some unknown reason, would not let the feelings from that time go – from the darkness and oppression to the uncertainty of not knowing what was happening around him, and the overarching fear of an uncertain future under the cloud of a scandal he had no hand in creating. This mélange of feelings compressed into a hardened point when the university administrator dropped the bombshell on him, transforming Murad into a completely different human being. For the first time in his life, he felt worthless, particularly after the director explained how limited his options were: he could resign to save face, and that would be the end of it, or he could allow the legal process to run its course – which could land him in prison and cost Murad his reputation and destroy his future.

"And, unfortunately, there are witnesses."

"Witnesses? Who?"

"Some of the nurses, some of your peers who have kept notes on your inappropriate behavior with some of your patients."

"Nurses? Peers? Like who?"

"Like Dr. Hadeel, for one."

Hadeel! In the whole world, Murad would never have imagined... not even in the most bizarre circumstance, that she would play a witness to a crime he had not committed. *There has to be some kind of mistake! Maybe this is a nightmare and I'll wake up now.* Murad pinched himself again and again trying to wake himself and end this farcical nightmare, but it clung to him no matter what he did.

"Director... there is some kind of mistake. There must be a mistake here. I did nothing of the sort. This is impossible." Murad paused a moment, trying to collect the thoughts, scattered like a flock of startled birds by the accusation. He stood quickly from the black leather chair in which he had been sitting and took the phone from his pocket.

"I'll call Hadeel right now. She'll tell you herself that this is a misunderstanding. That jackass married to her sister is making this up."

"Please, doctor! There is no call for slurs and name-calling. I've known Wajih Zakry for years. He is a respected businessman. Everyone knows he can be trusted."

Murad wasn't listening to what the director said. Every iota of his attention was focused on Hadeel's cell phone number, visible on the small screen. He hit the button to dial the number and put the handset to his ear.

When the line picked up, he burst out: "Hello, Hadeel." But the voice he heard was not hers.

"We're sorry. The number you have dialed cannot be reached at this time. Please try again."

"Doctor Murad, think this through. I will be waiting for your final response tomorrow. You can put a stop to this whole thing. A respected surgeon like you will be able to find work at any other hospital, I will write you a letter of recommendation myself. You just need to do the right thing. If you want to take this matter through the legal system, to open an investigation, of course, that is your right. If you do, however, I can make no promises about the outcome. If you just think about the news forums, when reports of an investigation leak out. You know how society will react to such a story."

It was settled then. One question remained for Murad, though. "What if?" "What if I hadn't resigned? What if I hadn't been paralyzed by fear like a hostage?" Despite the administrator's promise, there was no letter of recommendation. No hospital in Jeddah wanted him after word got out that a cosmetic and reconstructive surgeon had been forced to resign to avoid a scandal. Overnight, Murad went from being a skilled Saudi surgeon to one who was corrupt and outcast.

***

Fate. A mystery to some, ignored by others. What is fate? What secrets does it hold? Do we create our own destiny, or do we simply follow a fixed trajectory like a raindrop falling, or electricity through a steel bar, with no ability to alter the path?

These questions no longer bothered Murad as he made his way to the Elsaaidi International Hospital, his new workplace in Riyadh. They were, however, appropriate questions to ask at this moment, more than a year after the university incident. As people who survive tragedy sometimes do, he tried to find solace through gaining a greater and more complete understanding of the incident, to find some root cause that gave value to the tragedy, to glean from it some universal wisdom that would let him gain a bit of solace. The harder he tried to find a purpose behind what happened to him, though, the more he felt like there was no point to any of it; especially when all the hospitals he contacted in Jeddah to find a new job gave him the same answer. He never would have imagined this outcome, particularly when some of these facilities had been courting him in hopes of luring him to work for them, even part-time, just a few months earlier. They all refused him, and none of them would say why. He later learned that every hospital had received a letter from someone at the university, warning them that a certain doctor had been forced to retire because there was evidence that he had molested patients. It wasn't an official letter, but it cautioned them to protect their female patients from the clutches of a doctor who was "a ferocious dog who has turned his back on his calling and has not received due recompense for his heinous actions."

Things got worse every day. Murad started to feel like his life in Jeddah was strangling him. He thought about leaving the city where he had been born and raised. What was the use in staying in a place that was suffocating him, making him an outcast for his alleged crimes?

**

Murad continued his mental trek through time, following his memory to a rainy day in Jeddah when his mobile phone rang as he sat in his apartment in the Hamra district. He had made it his habit to turn on his phone just long enough to look at incoming text messages once a day. For some reason, he had failed to turn the phone off after he finished this time. Or did he? Maybe he just pressed the wrong button. He thought he had turned it off... or had he decided to leave it on that time? Regardless of the why of it, the result was that he got a call from his friend Barraa Alasili who wanted Murad to come for coffee at a shop near his house. Barraa was unconvinced by his attempts to turn him down with excuse after excuse; he insisted that his old friend come to see him. Murad even tried to beg off because of the pouring rain, rare in Jeddah, and the fact that it would cause road closures and traffic jams. It didn't help, Barraa wanted to see him over a steaming cup of coffee. Murad finally gave in to his friend and grudgingly left his apartment.

The roads were jammed, just as he had expected. Rainwater accumulated in the side streets near his building, forming small lakes, keeping cars from getting through. He tried a different route, but most outlets were closed. *I'm never going to get there like this.*

Murad decided to cancel the meeting, or at least postpone it until after the rain stopped and the roads dried up. He pulled his phone out and keyed in Barra's number.

"We're sorry, the number you are trying to reach…"

When he heard the familiar sound of the automated voice, he ended the call. He had a couple of options now, he could go back home – an attractive choice: he really did not want to keep the appointment with his friend – or he could keep making his way to the café, which really wasn't much further. At the time, Murad had no idea that this simple choice would change the course of his life. Go home, or go on? What to do. It seemed a trivial matter at the moment, no momentous outcome hanging delicately in the balance. Only later did he discover the importance packed into that choice; what he did next set the shape of his fate. The decision he made on that day led him to northern Riyadh and set him on the path to Elsaaidi Hospital.

***

Barraa couldn't come to the café because of the rain, but Murad ran into another friend there, one he had not seen for quite some time; a friend he had completely cut all ties with when he went to Canada to learn cosmetic surgery. A dear friend from childhood, his playmate for soccer games in the alleys, his after-school rival for the attention of girls, and his companion for any number of fishing trips on the Red Sea. Their estrangement didn't come because of the distance between Canada and Saudi Arabia, or the fact that his friend had enrolled in the Sharia Department despite earning grades in high school science that qualified him for medical school. It wasn't even because of the differences in their personalities after his friend became more religious and became a "seeker of knowledge." Even that did not erase the years they spent disagreeing over the friend's new lifestyle. Rather, a few months after Murad got to Montreal, he received news about his friend Nadim Alzoud that marked the turning point in their relationship: Nadim had been arrested because of a document addressed to the king asking for political reforms that he had signed along with a group of scholars and fellow seekers of knowledge. That's when Murad knew that the time had come to turn the page and focus on the present and future, and to stay away from political problems.

At first, Murad didn't recognize the clean-shaven man, redolent of fine cologne, calling to him from the opposite corner of the café. The man wore designer jeans and a purple shirt that was no less expensive than the jeans, and he appeared to be no more than thirty years old.

"Murad Qutuz! What a marvelous coincidence!"

This man, greeting him as warmly as one of his closest friends, had Murad stunned at first. He quickly recognized him, though, with their faces a few centimeters apart as he came in for a hug. From that distance, the features Murad had known more than fifteen years earlier came back to mind — it was Nadim before he became religious!

Was this the point at which everything shifted? The point that sets a path, determines the next twist? Or was it just one event that followed a series of others, a series that starts with a person's birth and ends with death, falling like dominoes with a preset pattern and direction with only one beginning and only one ending? When Murad ran into Nadim at the café on that rain-soaked day, these questions didn't come to mind at all. But a year and some change later, when the questions did surface, that hour-long meeting came to mind. He learned that after being freed from prison and granted permission to travel, Nadim had gone on to complete his university studies in the United States, earning a master's degree in international relations from the University of Washington. He stayed in the U.S. for a few years, working in a Middle East research center. His work there, along with a handful of reports and articles published in American and Arabic newspapers published in the U.S. and Lebanon, garnered him some level of fame. Nadim never mentioned what had happened to him while he was in prison, preferring to avoid talking about that period in his life. All he would say was jail gave him the chance to "think about a lot of things." Instead, Nadim spoke about his time after prison, and how he had drawn the attention of one of the most important businessmen in the world, Ghanim Elsaaidi, who brought him in as a media consultant and put him in charge of his media contacts and public relations for the whole massive, and massively diversified, commercial empire, one part of which was the largest hospital group in the Arab world and the Middle East.

"You mean the Elsaaidi Hospital group?" Murad asked after hearing that Nadim had ties to that massive medical establishment and its owner.

"Right, that's the one," Nadim said. "By the way, have you ever thought about relocating to Riyadh? The manager of the hospital there told me that they are looking for a new cosmetic surgeon."

Elsaaidi Hospital in Riyadh? Murad had reached out to hospitals in some of the Gulf states, in Canada, and the U.S. He hadn't thought to look at hospitals in Riyadh. The idea of living in that dusty city, in the middle of the Najd desert, a place he had only visited a handful of times on various errands, did not appeal to him much. To him, Saudi Arabia was Jeddah. Jeddah, the city where he could not find work. Jeddah, which had no room for him. Jeddah, where he had become an outcast.

He thought for a moment about what Nadim said. Elsaaidi Hospital. Riyadh... Why not? He had heard a lot about that hospital and the high salaries it paid. But should he tell Nadim what had happened to him? If the Elsaaidi Hospital administrator were to ask why he left the University Hospital in Jeddah, what should he say?

"Nadim, there is something I need to tell you about…"

Nadim smiled when he heard Murad's story. After a quiet moment, he said, "Forget Jeddah. Let's go to Riyadh."

***

The headache got worse during this trip down memory lane. Bad enough that Murad had to park his car in a gas station off the freeway. It was the last day of Ramadan, and he had not taken a single day off during the entire month, keeping the same schedule he did year-round. Working while fasting had never been a problem for him before, but he hadn't been sleeping well for the last several days because the recurring dream kept waking him. It left him constantly tired. That's why, when he saw the gas station, he decided to pull in. It wasn't that his car needed more fuel, it was just to stop and wait for the headache to lighten up a little. It was either this or break his fast by taking something for the pain.

Murad had just parked his car when he heard the car behind him blow its horn. There were four people inside, blaring the horn; it seemed he had inadvertently blocked that car's path. He moved his car a bit to let the car get around him to one of the gas pumps, waving his hand in apology. All he got in return was the driver's middle finger sticking up from the front window.

"Hey, Paki!" The driver shouted at the station attendant when he got out of the car with his companions. "Fill 'er up!" He lit a cigarette, shocking the attendant.

"Sir, you can no smoke this, it is danger for the gas, it will all set fire!"

"You God-damned Paki! You think you can tell me where to smoke?"

"What are you say? You no Muslim. You no morals!"

As the last word left the attendant's mouth, the smoker started punching and kicking him. One of his companions joined him in beating the attendant as the other two passengers watched, keeping the other attendants from coming to the aid of their fellow.

Murad was shocked by this tableau. He was even more shocked to see that it didn't end with just one blow or kick; they kept going, even after the poor attendant crumpled to the ground, telling them he surrendered. They kept kicking him, despite his cries for help.

After a moment's hesitation, Murad got out of his car and started towards the group. He looked around, looking for someone to help stop this fight, but he was the only one at the station apart from the four men, the prone attendant, and his fellow attendant who watched impotently.

"Hey, guys." He started to say, then one of the men turned on him with eyes burning for a fight.

"Listen, Chink, you'd better get back in your car and get out of here, or you'll get what this Paki is getting."

Murad stopped walking and looked around again, hoping to spot a police car or someone to help him through this ordeal he had stumbled on. But nothing had changed. He knew that he couldn't stand up to those guys, especially after one of them made an open threat. The brash one seemed serious about his warning. Now Murad had a choice: He could cast his lot and stay, try again to stop the clash with the poor worker, now knocked unconscious by the continuous kicks raining down on him, or he could leave this place and be content that he avoided being the target of those kicks.

The choice wasn't difficult for Murad. He chose safety. He chose to leave.

(2)
Headache

Something isn't right. Murad thought. The two tablets he took for the pain when the muezzin called out the sunset prayer weren't touching the headache. Was his body rebelling against him on the last day of Ramadan? *It's a year for rebellion. The whole world is rebelling in 2011. Take it easy. Why all this foolishness? Why does it all seem connected?* For a moment, he was struck by a strange thought – but it flew from his mind just as quickly – *how are this year's rebellions connected to these headaches?*

He sat on the couch in his office in the surgery wing, mildly nauseous. That was why he had decided to postpone the last operation. It was just a liposuction for a woman who was getting married in a little over a month. She wanted to make some improvements for her wedding, to be held in Paris this December. *There is still time before the end of the year. I'll postpone the surgery by a week or so. It won't be the end of the world.*

Murad didn't really like doing cosmetic surgery. His true passion was reconstructive surgery, and that's where he was at his best, particularly while he had been at the University Hospital in Jeddah. But here at the Elsaaidi Hospital, he was performing cosmetic surgeries.

Liposuctions, tummy tucks, botox injections, making lips look like Nancy Ajram's, noses like Haifa Wehbe's... These are the kinds of surgeries that make money in private practice. Reconstructive surgeries for burn victims or to repair disfigurement resulting from the removal of tumors and the like, they belong in government hospitals – they take a lot of effort and earn little money when compared to cosmetic surgery. Despite Murad's ambivalence about it, he was very good at cosmetic work. His reputation grew relatively quickly once he relocated to Riyadh. His skill earned him the admiration of patients desiring cosmetic enhancement as well as the envy of his peers in the profession. More important than either, however, was that performing cosmetic surgery brought Murad lots and lots of money.

***

The hospital cafeteria was practically empty because of the holiday break that started two days earlier. Most of the people who didn't take vacation had gone home to celebrate Iftar with their families. Murad was one of the few who stayed in the hospital.

When he entered the cafeteria, Charles Barton waved to him. Barton was the department head and had been called in to perform an emergency surgery. He invited Murad to sit with him.

"What have you been up to?" Asked Charles in a playful tone.

"What do you mean?"

"Haven't you gotten the call yet?"

33

Murad's brows knit in a bemused expression. His mobile phone rang right at that moment, as though the caller was waiting for Charles to ask; Murad's knit brows lifted in astonishment when he saw the number on his screen.

"Hello?"

"What's up, Murad? How could you cancel Badriya Zuwaini's case?" Nasser Alquwit, the hospital's CEO, growled through the phone.

Murad was a little confused, then he threw a pleading look to Charles, silently asking for help in his conundrum, but his partner at the table simply smiled.

Alquwit went on, not giving Murad a chance to respond, "Sheikh Ibrahim Assanduq just called me. He was furious about it."

"You have to perform operations as they are scheduled, Murad. I won't accept any excuses. If the surgery isn't done tonight, Sheikh Ibrahim threatened to complain to Sheikh Ghanim himself!"

"Sheikh Ibrahim Assanduq? You mean the famous prosecutor?"

"Yes, the famous prosecutor. He is also one of Sheikh Ghanim Elsaaidi's legal advisors. He owns this hospital; I think you may have heard of him."

Murad was not pleased by Alquwit's sarcasm.

"I'm sorry, but what does Sheikh Ibrahim have to do with Badriya Zuwaini? Is she related to him in some way?" For a moment, he thought the famous Sheikh might be the groom.

"She's his niece, his sister's daughter, and he dotes on her. Murad, I want you to drop whatever you're doing right now and prep for surgery. I won't accept anything less."

Nasser Alquwit hung up without allowing Murad to respond. He just gave the order, it was up to Murad to obey without hesitation. He had to perform the surgery, excuses would not be tolerated. He had to suck out that fat. The bride's body must be modified!

"I can't focus! It's this headache!" he wanted to shout. "It is just liposuction, not a kidney transplant! What harm would come from postponing it until after the holiday?" But he didn't shout. He just covered his face with his hands.

"Are you OK?" Charles asked, noticing the stress in his table companion.

"Bad headache. That's why I wanted to postpone the surgery."

"Sorry about that. I tried to tell you that Nasser called me a moment ago to ask why you had canceled, but he beat me to you. Anyway, don't worry about it. Eat. Then go on home. Don't worry about the surgery."

"I don't want to cause trouble. I'll take some more pain medicine. I'm sure that will make the headache a bit better, and I'll be able to perform the surgery."

A thin, dark-skinned young man approached with a tray carrying a glass of Vimto. He put the juice on the table. He mildly asked Murad, speaking with a Tunisian accent, if he wanted anything else. Murad looked at the waiter to say thanks, but the headache suddenly exploded and this time he lost control. The pain was unbearable. He tried to get up but collapsed to the floor instead. For some reason, he gestured at the waiter as though he wanted something, or maybe he wanted the waiter to leave him. Murad tried to speak, he tried to spit out a few words, but darkness soon overcame him.

(3)
Elusive Memories

The screams of the women filled the air as their men were cut down one after the other. Even the children weren't safe from the slaughter. The only thing Murad could do was look around himself. He had no idea what was going on or why he couldn't move – the whole situation was incomprehensible. Everyone around him was running in sheer panic, not paying any attention to him. It was as though he wasn't there at all. There was one middle-aged man with a thick black beard and pale, ruddy skin who was looking at him. Murad realized something that he had missed up to that point: he was dreaming. It was the same dream he had experienced from time to time throughout his whole life. This time, however, he was aware of the fact that he was dreaming. How could it be so? How could someone know that they were dreaming during the dream? Suddenly, he was transported to another, more familiar scene. He was with his father in a remote village, standing in front of a small building that looked like it might be a house. Where was this place? Then he felt the world around him start to fade, or maybe he was the one fading away! It was unclear which was which until he felt himself waking from a deep slumber.

"Doctor Murad, hi. Try not to exert yourself. Don't try to get out of bed! Please!" The emergency room nurse took him by the arm and called for her partner to come help. "You are in the emergency room. You had a severe case of hypoglycemia. Maybe you didn't stay up and have enough to eat last night, then you worked too hard today. You should have had some juice as soon as the muezzin cried sunset."

Juice. The Vimto the waiter was bringing, the thin, dark-skinned man. Murad remembered what happened now; he had fainted suddenly right after the headache intensified. He knew that he wasn't dreaming. He was back to reality, in the Elsaaidi International Hospital, where he worked.

"You're alright now. Dr. Bakhit ordered another blood glucose check, just to be sure your levels are back to normal."

Murad nodded in agreement. The nurse offered him a smile, releasing his arm so she could get the meter for measuring his glucose level. Just as she left, Dr. Charles appeared, still wearing his scrubs as he had just come to check on Murad.

"Excellent, excellent. You look much better now."

"Sorry, Charles. I don't know how this happened. I'm feeling much better now. I think I can perform the Badriya surgery."

Charles cut him off, "Don't even think about that silly operation. I want you to go home and get some rest. Don't think about surgery – your health is more important. Lady Badriya's fat can wait a few more days.

tonight!"

Murad smiled his thanks. Not only did Charles get him out of hot water with the hospital's CEO, but he also offered to drive Murad home when the ER doctor refused to let him drive himself after his sudden fainting spell.

***

The housing development where Murad lived wasn't far from the hospital, but the roads were packed at that time of the night – evening prayer had just finished, and the mosques had just disgorged the massive amount of people who had waited until the last minute, as usual, to fulfill the holiday's religious obligations. Murad silently contemplated the skyscrapers and buildings around him, feeling like he was seeing them for the first time. Ever since he woke from his blackout, it was as though everything around him was slightly off. He couldn't shake the odd feeling that something had changed. He didn't know what it was, or how it had changed, but something was not the same as it had been. Something wasn't right.

"Are you going to the party tomorrow?" Charles asked. Ghanim Elsaaidi held an Eid party every year in the Al-Khuzama district, he always invited the high-level employees from his various businesses and organizations, Muslims and non-Muslims alike, along with his partners and some of Saudi Arabia's most influential figures.

"Maybe. I haven't decided yet."

The invitation had come to him through Sarah Alquwit, Ghanim Elsaaidi's wife, in thanks for the good work he had done on her face, erasing no small number of years.

"I'm going. This is one of the few chances I get to get my hands on some excellent French wine in this country!" Charles told him with a wink. "The worst thing at the party is Nasser. Oh, how I hate that man! He's the worst CEO I've seen at any hospital; his most important qualification is being the brother to the wife of the man who owns the hospital he directs!"

"I've noticed that you're always at odds with him. Is he really that bad?"

Charles gaped at him. "As though you don't know. Yes, he really is that bad! He isn't qualified to be CEO of a grocery store, much less a facility as large as the Elsaaidi International Hospital! Do you know how many times I turned in my resignation? I lost count, that's how many times. I withdrew it each time because Sheikh Ghanim asked me to. I remember this one time when Dr. Butler – he was chair of the kidney transplant department – retired. Nasser wanted to bring an American surgeon to take his place; the man he picked had been forced to resign from a famous academic hospital in the U.S. Imagine, the man had lost his license to practice. He wasn't allowed to do kidney transplants in the U.S. before he came to Saudi Arabia, because he had been manipulating the patient waiting list. Meanwhile, I had turned in the resume of an excellent Saudi doctor who had trained with one of my friends in Chicago. Nasser didn't want him; he had made up his mind to hire this quack! The whole thing nearly drove me crazy. I asked him why he was so dead-set on hiring a bad foreign surgeon over an excellent surgeon from his own country, one who I was certain would develop the department and raise its reputation. Do you know what he said?"

"What did he say?"

"He told me not to be more Saudi than the Saudis."

"But it looks like he did what you asked. The chair of the kidney transplant center is Bandar Alyaaqoub."

"He didn't do it willingly. He was forced to."

"How so?"

"I had to do something I never wanted to resort to, even if it is something you Saudis are accustomed to," Charles said with a smirk, letting Murad in on his teasing.

"What are you talking about?" Murad asked.

Charles looked at Murad again, then shook his head in wonder. "Personal connections! I took the whole thing to Sheikh Ghanim. I told him that I couldn't work at a hospital that would bring in quack physicians to take the jobs of all the people who couldn't find work at home! When he asked me for an alternative, I told him about Bandar Alyaaqoub – Sheikh Ghanim sent the order to have him appointed."

Murad was shocked by Charles' story. He hadn't known anything about the conditions under which Bandar had gotten the job some two years earlier. Bandar had been one of the first people he had gotten to know in Riyadh when he moved here.

"As far as I'm concerned, the most important things I accomplished that year were signing the papers to appoint Bandar, and signing the papers that brought you on board. The hospital gained two Saudi doctors who are at the top of their fields."

That last sentence gave Murad pause. He didn't come on board the same year as Bandar. Maybe Charles had mixed the papers up in his mind, maybe he meant some other doctor who was hired that year and the dates just got confused in the elderly American surgeon's memory. That's what Murad chalked it up to, in any case.

(4)

Unfamiliar Turns

"The Syrian people are preparing to vote in the middle of next month on the proposed constitutional amendment. It is expected to pass, and the Syrian government will no longer be a republic, it will become a constitutional monarchy under the rule of the Assad family."

Something about that story drew Murad's attention as he watched the morning news on the day of Eid. It seemed to him that he remembered something completely different; his memories from before weren't the same as what was being broadcast on the television now. He spent some time thinking about how closely he followed world events. When he tried to recall the last news broadcast he watched or newspaper he read, he found that he hadn't done either for a long time. Maybe that's why the events he saw or heard seemed out of sync with his expectations. He was starting to worry about himself when he walked to his garage only to find it empty. He remembered then that he had left his car at the hospital the night before. He was a bit annoyed, now he would have to find a cab to take him from home to the hospital where his car was parked. His only option was to take a short walk over to the nearby gas station on Rais Street. Maybe he could find an available taxi there. "What a morning!"

***

It was hot and dusty outside, making the walk to the gas station entirely unpleasant. He looked at the houses around him, ranging from medium-sized villas to small palaces. Most of the people in those homes were sleeping as their drivers washed the cars with hoses, the dirty water draining to the middle of the road and flowing until it pooled up in one of the many potholes that dotted the neighborhood.

Since moving to the neighborhood, Murad had never made it a habit to walk. It had been since... "Since when? When did I move here?" For some reason, Murad couldn't recall the date on which he had moved to Riyadh. At least, he was confused about it. He stopped suddenly when he reached a side street heading north from where he stood. He had planned to go that way to Rais Street where the gas station was. The side street wasn't the street he had been headed for. He looked at the houses around him. They seemed a little different. The street seemed a bit off, too. There was a different side street at the end of the road, not Rais Street. Murad scratched his head, astonished and concerned by the gaps in his memory that had started to increase of late. Then he kept walking.

After taking several unfamiliar turns, Murad made it to the gas station. He went straight to the shop to buy a bottle of water to slake his thirst and rehydrate after his

44

sweaty walk that had gone on much longer than he anticipated on such a hot day. When he got to the door, he saw the shop was closed. *Of course! It's the first day of Eid!*

"It is early for work."

Murad spun to look at the man addressing him. It was the same Bengali worker who had received the beating the day before. There were contusions and abrasions on his face. Murad didn't expect to see him at this gas station. *What brought him here?* But when he looked around, it was the same one he had stopped at yesterday. He must have had walked a long way from home, towards the hospital, but the walk didn't seem to have taken that long.

"Thanks." He said, then, a bit hesitantly, he asked, "Did you get checked out by a doctor? I mean, after what happened to you yesterday?"

The worker smiled but didn't answer. He just looked at Murad who stood there, embarrassed to be standing across from the man he hadn't been able to help during the violent episode. For a moment, he wished the worker would curse him or blame him for not helping instead of just painting this cold smile on his thin, dark face. He wanted to scream at the worker, "There is nothing to smile about!"

"Did you or the station owner report those guys? I'm sure they live around here. I think I saw the car they drove parked at one of these houses."

He wasn't really sure of what he said about where they lived or their car, but he felt a strong desire to break the uncomfortable silence, even if it meant saying something that was more conjecture than actual fact.

"Allah saw it all." The Bengali man answered. "No need to report." Then he went to a cab parked next to one of the pumps.

Just for a moment, Murad thought about following him, apologizing, maybe giving him some money. But he didn't. Instead, he left, looking for a cab other than the one the Bengali worker was filling with gas.

(5)
Sarah

Unlike the morning, Riyadh's streets were packed in the evening. Murad had no idea it would take him so long to drive from his house to Ghanim Elsaaidi's palace in the Al-Khuzama District; it took him forty minutes, if not more. More than once as he drove, he thought about giving up on the whole idea of attending the party and going home to spend the evening alone watching television. Just as he got to the next exit that would take him back to the Al-Rawdah district, he got a message on his phone:

Don't be late, I'm waiting for you

He was shocked to see the name "Sarah" on the address line. When he added patients and coworkers to his address book, he normally added their full names. When the listing only had the first name, it was a signal to him that they were friends or family. Sarah Alquwit was neither.

Murad tried to remember how many operations he had performed on her. Three, maybe four? He had performed a facelift, breast enlargement, a nose job, and liposuction. It had to be four, then, but it also seemed like there may have been more than that. *In less than a year, though? How?* His memory wasn't making sense. His memories of events were overlapping in a way he had never experienced. It felt like he had the memories of two or more people crammed into his head. Even his familiarity with events and locations were fuzzy. He was absent-mindedly driving to Ghanim Elsaaidi's palace as though he had been there many times, despite knowing that he had never been there. But how?

The fact that he hadn't asked anyone for a map dawned on him for the first time, but it wasn't just that – he didn't think about how he would get there at all. When he got in the car to go to the Al-Khuzama district, he didn't even think about it, he just went. How could he know the way to a place he had never been before? It wasn't as though he could have gone and forgotten about it. Murad started to worry about himself again. *I know I've never been to Sheikh Ghanim's palace.* That made him doubt the route he was following. He had to be going the wrong way. For just a moment he felt an urge to pick up his phone and call Charles or Nadim and ask for directions, but he didn't. Instead, he found himself in a queue of cars waiting at the gate of a large palace overlooking the Wadi Hanifa oasis. The doubt was gone, he had arrived at his destination.

(6)

A Palace within the City

When someone enters the grounds of Ghanim Elsaaidi's palace for the first time, they can't help but gape at the scenery in amazement. The property was nothing at all like the environment outside; guests to the grounds see a rich garden surrounding a large pond, a small stream flowing out of one end and winding its way around the residential building. From there, it was impossible to remember that one was still in the middle of a dry desert city, constantly suffering from a shortage of water. The impression one had upon entering was of being magically transported to a completely different world from the one outside. The concrete road changed to cobblestones at the exterior gates; rumor said the stones had been imported from France. Driving in, the transition felt like one had turned on to an old European road. The 500 meters from the gate to where the road turned and crossed a bridge over the stream was lined with oak and fig trees, then it ended at a circular drive in front of the residence, which itself looked like a miniaturized version of a French palace from the Middle Ages, complete with marble carvings and pillars. Though the Elsaaidi palace was smaller in size, it was more luxurious and charming. It was probably this aspect of it that convinced a visitor that the rumors that the palace had cost at least a billion Saudi Riyals to build were likely true. Even this was a pittance next to Forbes' report of Ghanim Elsaaidi's net worth when the magazine listed the richest people in the world; he topped the list with a fortune of over $100 billion.

***

Murad parked his car under an oak tree decorated with lights next to a footpath along the palace's lake. This was the closest parking spot he found with all the cars that had arrived at the annual party before him. Each year the party was packed with men and women wearing their finest. There was a servant beside the door waiting to collect keys from the guests who did not have private drivers. On the other side was a female attendant, there to take the ladies' wraps. Murad had no sense that he was a stranger here. Everything seemed familiar, as though he had been to the palace many times. He even knew which way to go inside the building, heading for the main hall without hesitation, like he was following a habit, almost like he lived there. The feeling faded quickly, though, when that agonizing headache came back, forcing him to stop where he was – next to a bench with silk upholstery, just outside the hall.

A voice spoke up behind him, "Murad, are you alright?" Charles had just come in as well. "You seem a bit out of sorts. Has your headache come back?"

"Yeah, it seems like it has. But I thought it might, so I brought some pain killers with me."

"Good. I'm worried about this recurring headache of yours. You seem to be suffering from it frequently lately. After the Eid break, you should go see one of the neurologists to try and find out what is causing it."

"It's no big deal, there's no need for…" but Murad couldn't finish his sentence. The headache had ratcheted up another notch and all he could do was hold his head in his hands.

"Dr. Murad, are you alright?" A waiter asked as he approached the pair with a tray of refreshments.

"Mohamed, could you get Dr. Murad a glass of water?"

"Certainly, of course. Right away."

No sooner had the waiter scrambled off than the headache started to fade. Murad rubbed at his face and wiped away the sweat. Self-conscious about his appearance, Murad quickly made his way to a side hall where he found the door to a guest bathroom. No one was there but him, though Charles trailed behind him having followed from the bench.

"Murad, this is getting serious. We don't have to keep quiet about…"

Murad cut him off as he splashed his face with cold water from the tap. "That waiter. Is he the same guy who works at the hospital?"

"What difference does a waiter make right now? Don't try to change the subj…"

"Please, Charles!" Murad shouted. "Just answer the question!"

For a moment, the old American doctor stood in silent shock at his tone. He had never heard Murad speak so sharply before.

"Yes, he is. You seem to be better now. If you'll excuse me, I should go offer my greetings to Sheikh Ghanem. I'll head over to the West Hall after, like usual. I'll see you there."

Murad slumped in shame as he watched Charles leave stiffly. He wanted to apologize, but his friend was already gone.

Sitting on a marble bench next to the sink, Murad actually did feel noticeably better; the headache had completely vanished, as though it had never been there. The young waiter was on his mind, now that he had seen him a second time. His dark, thin face was familiar, as though he had encountered him several times before. Charles seemed to know him well. Had he been working at the hospital cafeteria for a long time without Murad noticing? *Impossible*, Murad thought, *I never forget a face*. Particularly if the young man had been waiting on him for a while. *My God! What's happening to me? Do I have early-onset Alzheimer's? Am I losing my mind?*

"Murad? Are you alright? Mohamed told me what happened."

Sarah Alquwit came into the restroom, clearly concerned, carrying a glass of water for Murad. Her brother Nasser was with her.

"Thanks." Now embarrassed, he washed down two pills with the water. "Just a headache. It's not the first time."

"But you look so pale." Sarah pressed her right palm to Murad's forehead, catching him completely off-guard. He wasn't expecting her to do anything like that, particularly with her brother standing there, though he seemed completely indifferent to her behavior and to Murad's condition.

"I'm alright, Mrs. Sarah," Murad said, confused, removing the hand of Sheikh Ghanim's wife from his head.

"Mrs. Sarah?" The lady of the manor broke out in peals of laughter after repeating the moniker Murad gave her. "You are definitely not well. What happened? Are you embarrassed in front of Nasser?" Sarah leaned in and planted a quick kiss on Murad's lips.

"Would you like to rest for a bit in the guest room?"

"No!" Murad replied quickly, "I'm fine!" He felt like he was about to lose his mind. Why would she kiss him like that, and in front of her brother? The whole situation was becoming a confused mess to him.

"Alright. I'm headed to the west hall; I'll wait for you there. Don't make me wait too long. And try not to spend too much time with Ghanim and his guests this time. See you there."

She surprised him with another kiss before she turned and left along with her brother, who did not seem surprised at all; unlike Murad, who stood rooted to the spot, not sure what just happened.

(7)
The Conundrum

O ne of the rules Ghanim Elsaaidi learned on his journey to accumulate great wealth was that money is not enough by itself. It must be paired with prestigious social status; doing so adds a bit of momentum to the money. Moreover, this status must not be local in scope; it must be recognized regionally as well as internationally. With this understanding, Elsaaidi was extremely careful to project the image of a man of action with clean hands; generous, the perfect image of social responsibility expressed through his charitable projects, not only in his home country but in all nations – Muslim and non-Muslim alike. He also engaged in cultural activities, which were no less important than the charitable efforts. He founded a cultural center with a goal of supporting Arabic literary endeavors, and he established several cultural prizes that bore his name. And, of course, he did not neglect the religious aspect. He poured out millions every year to build and maintain mosques in many cities and villages, and he was known for aiding poor students of religion. This aspect of his social work was very important to Sheikh Ghanim. He firmly believed that appearance always trumped substance in Arab societies in general, especially among the Gulf States. He was sure he could do whatever he wanted in his private life as long as he maintained the appropriate façade, one that toed the line of perfunctory traditional expectations. So his parties celebrating religious holidays were segregated: in the official hall, the guests were advisors, high-ranking employees from his companies, partners from Saudi Arabia and abroad, and other influential figures he had social or business ties to. In the ballroom at the western corner of the palace, the atmosphere was less formal and more fun. Only special guests were allowed there, those who welcomed and wanted a more liberal atmosphere than that which ruled over the formal hall, where talk of politics, business, and, at times, philosophy and science reigned, particularly when his American partner, Virginia Tabt, was in attendance.

***

"Is anyone on the planet today smarter than her?" That was the question printed on the cover of Time magazine several years ago over a photo of Virginia Tabt, giving the impression that she was the one asking the question. Her incredible skills were not the only basis for the headline, though they had been fodder for newspaper articles and reports since her adolescence. She had enrolled at Harvard at 13 and earned a Ph.D. in physics and biochemistry at 20, to say nothing of her mastery of seven languages or her score of 200 on an IQ test at ten years of age, 20% higher than Albert Einstein! That was when her incredible brilliance earned her first place in a national competition for science and creativity held in Seattle. That award, coupled with the scholarship from Harvard, made everyone anticipate incredible academic achievements in her future. She spent several years working as an assistant professor at Princeton after graduating; all the while delivering public lectures written for a lay audience. Her lectures were so popular that the BBC turned them into documentaries about the miracles of science and the discoveries that disrupted human concepts about how the universe works as seen through the lens of the theory of relativity and quantum physics. The documentaries included contemporary scientific developments around the world and the latest theories in physics that tried to connect the four forces of nature through string theory and superstring theory. When she turned 30, Tabt suddenly decided to leave academia and move into the commercial world, using a small amount of capital to establish a biotech firm.

The press had perked up and paid attention back then because she had partnered with a group of international businessmen led by Ghanim Elsaaidi. During the interview for the cover story, Time magazine asked her what brought one of the richest men in the world together with one of the smartest women in the world. Her pithy reply was:

"So we can give birth to a new world, unlike anything humans have witnessed before!"

***

"What you say is impossible. The rules of life are fixed. If they weren't, everything would become chaos."

Sheikh Ibrahim Assanduq's response was heated; Victoria was, as usual, provoking him with philosophical perspectives influenced by her scientific background. As agitated, and often even angry, as Sheikh Ibrahim could be, she was the perfect image of calm. She gave him as much time as he wanted to express how much he disagreed with her opinion, never interrupting, waiting until he was done talking. Then she would continue, countering his rejoinders, which would make him even angrier. He thought of getting up and just leaving the session many times and would have done so if he did not fear the possible insult to their host, who was enthralled by their banter.

"Sheikh Ibrahim," came Victoria's response evenly in Arabic, "I agree with you. The rules of life are fixed. However, our understanding of these rules... well. That's what changes. For example, a hundred years ago or so, people believed that time was immutable and flowed in only one direction. When Einstein proved that this view was incorrect, that time is a fourth dimension not unlike space, and that time is relative... that time passes differently from the point of view of a moving person than it does for someone sitting still in proportion to the speed at which the person is moving – the faster they go, the slower time moves. This is a scientific fact, proven by experimentation, but many people don't know about it because it isn't visible in the normal world where things move at speeds that are extremely slow when compared to the speed of light. This is one clear example of how observed reality and factual reality may not be the same thing. But there is something even more astounding: according to quantum physics, the entire world is based on probability, not on certainty. It is possible to verify anything, no matter how strange that thing might seem. It is just a matter of probability. The probability could be slight, or it could be great; the difference sets the course of everyday life."

"Nonsense! How could everything be subject to probability? As if there is no such thing as cause and effect. What you say defies the simplest rules of logic. If everything is under the tyranny of probability, it would mean that the probability exists that this tea I'm drinking will become coffee." Sheikh Ibrahim scoffed, bringing laughter from a few of the guests.

"Esteemed Sheikh, if you want coffee, we'll make you some rather than have you wait for your tea to change. If we don't, my dear Sheikh, you could be waiting for quite some time." Ghanim Elsaaidi injected, drawing even more laughter from the guests.

"According to quantum mechanics, it is within the scope of possibility for your tea to turn into coffee. Possible, it is just a matter of probability. The probability is, however, extremely small, it might happen once in a billion years. That is why we don't see such things in our day-to-day experiences. On the other hand, superstring theory says that it could happen in a world parallel to our own."

"Virginia, now you're carrying us off into the world of fantasy and marvels; this isn't hard science anymore." Sheikh Ghanim said lightly.

"While it might sound like a fairy tale or science fiction, it is squarely in the domain of current physics research. In fact, the world we could see, starting a hundred years ago, through the lens of relativity and quantum theory – and we are now starting to glimpse through superstring theory - is not the one most people believe in." She answered.

"For myself," Sheikh Ibrahim asserted hotly, "I do not believe in these theories. They make people doubt their own reality and everything around them. As though there has been nothing absolute for human beings to believe in since the creation of Adam, Allah's peace be upon him! These theories do nothing but help those who advocate atheism. That's why our youth today go astray, they've lost their confidence in everything because of these kinds of theories, which are followed quickly by other theories, even if they are shortly invalidated!"

"Science searches for facts. It has nothing to do with people's going astray or not. And, I'm sorry, Sheikh Ibrahim, but who said there are any kinds of constraints to how people understand this life? Such limitations are nothing more than mythology, concocted by a few people in order to pass their convictions on to others."

"Oh, Allah, give us strength! What do you mean, there are no constants? What about human values? I won't even say "Islamic" values, I know full well that you aren't Muslim, and so…"

Sheikh Ghanim interrupted firmly, worried that the discussion was starting down a path he didn't want it to follow. "Mind yourself, Sheikh Ibrahim. Virginia's religion is a personal issue; we do not want this dialog to become an accounting of religion. It would be better to just stop now."

"Sheikh Ibrahim's question has some merit, and he has the right to be shocked by what I said," Virginia told Sheikh Ghanim with a smile to let him know that not only was she not upset, she wanted to continue. "Sheikh Ibrahim, please allow me to explain what I meant using a simple thought experiment. Imagine that you were trapped on the roof of a building and you found a bomb, moments from exploding. You only have two choices in the time left: either the bomb explodes on the roof, killing you, or you throw the bomb down to the street and another man dies; it is his own bad luck that he happened to be under that building at that moment. What would you do in this situation? Let it blow up and take you with it, or throw it, causing someone else to die?"

"This is hypothetical. I don't have to answer." The sheik said, showing his discomfort with Virginia's question.

"I know it's hypothetical. I told you it was a thought experiment. It will clarify the concept quite well, but you'll have to play along; if you don't, there's no point to the discussion."

"Answer her, Sheikh Ibrahim. I'd throw the bomb down to the street, myself. I value nothing more than I value myself." Ghamin said. Several of the guests who were listening nodded in agreement, including Ghanim's media advisor, Nadim Alzoud.

Ibrahim finally conceded, "I agree with Sheikh Ghanim. I would throw the bomb off the building and pray for forgiveness for myself and ask Allah to accept the other man as a martyr."

"Excellent. That's what most people would do. But please allow me to make the circumstances a little more complex. What if there was more than one person on the ground under the building? Two people, for example. What would you do now? Would you throw the bomb? Is your life worth the lives of two others?"

"There is no easy answer. I thank Allah that I've never been in such a situation, forced to make a decision like that."

"I'd throw the bomb. Who cares." This time, it was Nadim who spoke up and got a laugh from the people around them.

"What if it was more than two? Three? Four? Ten? At what point would you change your mind and say that your life was worth less than theirs combined?" She paused, "Let's change the scenario a bit. This time, Sheikh Ibrahim, just answer without thinking: what if you could throw the bomb off the right side of the building and kill one, or the left side and kill two? What side would you chose?"

"The right side, of course. Better one should die than two." Sheikh Ibrahim's answer came confidently this time.

"Even if the one person was Muslim, and the two were not?"

Silence fell over the whole group for a few moments in the aftermath, no one there expected this embarrassing question. Sheikh Ghanim spoke up:

"Virginia, I really don't understand what you are getting at with these hypotheticals."

"It isn't actually hypothetical at all." Virginia went on. "These decisions are made every day all over the world. All I've done is put it in plain language; that's what has made everyone uncomfortable. Do you know, however, that worldwide expenditures on a cure for AIDS are over 15 billion dollars, while only a billion and a half go to malaria? Keep in mind that there are about thirty million people around the world who have AIDS, while more than two hundred million have malaria. Both diseases are fatal. The world has decided to drop the bomb on the people with malaria in order to save the people with AIDS. Isn't it so? Their reasoning is clear: a person in the West is more likely to contract AIDS than malaria. Just as a person might value his life more than the lives of others, he will value the lives of his clan members more than those of other clans. It doesn't stop there. This kind of decision is made around many different issues. Take the priorities used for budgeting as an example. Every riyal or dollar or euro spent on one issue, in the end, comes at the expense of something else. No matter how much we have, there is a limit. And that is where the question comes in: by what moral standard do we make such decisions?"

Silence fell over the group again. No one wanted to follow that or try to refute her statement, especially when they all knew how well Virginia was able to rebut arguments and give explanations backed up with facts and figures to support her opinions. Everyone, including Sheikh Ibrahim, knew that debating Virginia was a losing battle, so they all kept quiet.

(8)

A Few Moments Earlier

"**M**ohamed?" Sarah Alquwit called out to the waiter as he walked quickly by, carrying a glass of water. "Do you know if Doctor Murad has arrived yet?"

"Yes, he just arrived. He doesn't seem well, though."

"He's not well? What do you mean?" Sarah asked with concern she did not bother to disguise.

"I saw him holding his head like he had a terrible headache. Dr. Charles was with him and asked me to bring him some water."

Sarah took the glass from Mohamed and asked, "Where is he now?"

"I saw him heading to the side restroom."

Sarah hurried off in the direction the waiter said Murad had gone, taking the water with her. As she turned into the appropriate hallway, her brother Nasser happened upon her.

"Sarah, I need you for something important."

"Not now."

"It can't wait, and it won't take long. I want you to convince Ghanim to put Wajih in charge of the hospital expansion, and it would be best to take care of it tonight."

"Why tonight?"

"Wajih is coming down from Jeddah for the party. I promised him we'd get the signature tonight, tomorrow at the latest."

Sarah looked at her brother, her dark eyes filled with disbelief and anger.

"And who allowed you to invite that man? You know perfectly well that I cannot stand him. Oh my God, Nasser! You're stressing me out!"

"Sarah, please." He said, "the project is worth half a billion riyals!"

"And you'll get a commission, of course. Like always."

"Sarah…"

"Alright." She was quiet for a moment. "Consider the project his, on the condition that you do not bring him to the Western Hall. I do not want to see him! I swear, if it weren't for how much I respect his wife, Dr. Hadeel, I wouldn't let a man like that into the palace at all. We have to take the bad with the good, I suppose."

Sarah hurriedly stepped towards the bathroom, but Nasser blocked the way again.

"Where are you rushing off to?"

"Murad isn't well. It sounds like his headache is back again. I want you to run every possible test on him tomorrow."

"We're off tomorrow, maybe after…"

Sarah cut him off, "I said tomorrow! Even if you have to call the doctors in from their graves!" She started walking again.

"Sarah, wait a sec. There was something else I wanted to talk to you about."

She stopped and turned towards him. She could tell from the way he hesitated what he wanted to talk about, particularly since he had broached the subject before. "What is it?"

"Murad... your relationship with him..."

"Stop right there." Sarah cut her brother off, rage coloring her voice and visible on her face, which had been the picture of serene beauty only a moment before. She suddenly seemed very intimidating. "I swear, Nasser if you dare mention my relationship with Murad again; if you even think of sticking your nose into things that don't concern you, it will not end well for you!"

"I... I just... I'm worried about you."

"You don't need to be afraid for me, I know perfectly well what I'm doing. You should worry about yourself, brother, and pay attention to your own situation – that foul order you're smelling? It's coming from you."

"If this is about my commission, I am grateful to you for everything." Nasser was clearly confused by what his sister had just said, seemingly out of nowhere.

"I'm not talking about the commission," Sarah told him with a malevolent smile.

"What do you mean then?"

"I'm talking about the director of patient relations. She's lovely, isn't she? What's her name?" She obviously knew the woman's name; she was just toying with him. "Ah, yes. I remember. Dina Elsawiyi. Right?"

Taken aback, Nasser wondered how she could know. He had been so careful to keep it a secret. Hadn't he taken every possible precaution?

"Those are just rumors." He said.

"Nasser, please. Don't try to outsmart me. Did you really think, even for a moment, that something would happen around me that I don't know about? If you did, you don't know me very well, little brother. Now, let me go check on Murad. As a matter of fact, why don't you come with me? You can check on him yourself."

Without waiting for his answer, Sarah turned her back on her brother and headed to the bathroom where Murad was. She knew Nasser's only option was to follow her so he could check on her lover, or at least pretend to, under duress.

(9)
Confusion

All Murad wanted to do was leave the party, particularly after what Nasser Alquwit had just seen. The whole thing was a farce. What made Sarah, wife to Ghanim Elsaaidi, behave in such an inappropriate way? Even more astounding was her brother's silence, watching them as though it were the most natural thing and he was completely accustomed to it – and didn't think anything was wrong. How would he face Sheikh Ghanim? That got him thinking about what might happen if he knew. But more important, what was the meaning of her behavior? There was nothing between Murad and Sarah; she was just a client; he had done a few plastic surgeries on her, just like many others. *Have I done something to make her think there is more to it than that?* He started going over the times he had been around her in his mind. It was always at the hospital... but he had also met her here at the palace, or maybe other places... his memories began to double and overlap, full of conflicting events. *Oh my God! What has happened to me?*

"Murad! Murad!" The voice called from behind as he crossed the palace threshold. "Where are you going?

"Nadim. I was… I…" Murad didn't know quite how to answer.

"I bumped into Charles a few minutes ago. He told me what happened."

"What do you mean? Nothing happened!" Murad answered defensively.

"The headache. What's going on? Are you alright?" Nadim asked, gripping Murad's shoulder and steering him back inside. "Come on. Everyone's been asking about you."

"Everyone?"

"You missed Virginia's chat with Sheikh Ibrahim! I thought for sure he was going to take off his shoe and throw it at her!" Nadim laughed, ignoring the shock on Murad's face. "No one here can match wits with Virginia like you. Without you there, the conversation just isn't the same."

"Nadim, what are you talking about? What do I have to do with such things?

Nadim stopped suddenly and closely examined his friend's face. Then he laughed, long and loud.

"You're kidding me, right? This is one of your vicious jokes, isn't it? No, no. You won't fool me this time. I'm not Charles, poor fellow." Nadim laughed again as he drew Murad into the main hall, paying no heed to the surprise evident on his companion's face.

*   *   *

After shaking hands with the guests, Murad sat near Virginia who spoke to him warmly, though he still couldn't understand why. Even Ghanim Elsaaidi drew him into the conversation from time to time, as did several guests – but not Sheikh Ibrahim, who appeared to be somewhat angry with him.

"Why so quiet, my dear Sheikh?" Ghanim teased. "I hope you aren't still angry with Dr. Murad for not operating on your niece himself."

"It would appear, Sheikh Ghanim, that my family isn't good enough for the doctor." Sheikh Ibrahim said, making no attempt to hide the bitterness in his voice.

"No, nothing could be further from the truth. Dr. Murad cares for your family just as he does for all." Nadim answered lightly to calm the waters, particularly since he had noticed his friend seemed unusually slow-witted. Less than half an hour later, it was clear that something was wrong. Murad was not usually so quiet, and when he did speak, he barely uttered a few words, like he didn't know what to say.

"Are you overstressed tonight? You aren't... I don't know how to describe it. You aren't your usual self."

Murad saw his opportunity to excuse himself. "Yes. I'm very tired, I think it might be best if I..."

But Nadim didn't give him a chance to finish his sentence. "I know what'll perk you right up and pull you out of this funk. They'll call us to dinner in a few minutes, then we can head over to the other hall. Same as me, you need to cut loose a bit. It's Eid!"

Murad didn't know what Nadim meant by cutting loose, but it was actually only a few minutes before the call to dinner came. Instead of going to the dining hall with the other guests, he found himself walking away from the hall with his friend, towards the ballroom at the west end of the palace.

(10)
The West Side

Absolutely insane! For someone to be in a place like this and not enjoy everything on offer! Charles told himself, Everything about this party is beautiful. The main hall had balconies overlooking the back garden that sloped down to a fair-sized lake, the view no less breathtaking than the garden in front of the palace. The musical ensemble played jazz from the 1920s, fine red wine dazzled his taste buds, and there were ladies in attendance, shimmering in their gowns and revealing evening dresses. Everything at the party was amazing. The best part was how it combined to create an atmosphere that reminded him of the stories he had heard and read about the United States during the jazz age, before the Great Depression, during the Prohibition when people would surreptitiously drink at parties in the mansions of the wealthy. The atmosphere was redolent of his homeland's history, filled with a sense of adventure and an appetite for living with no regard for the future; it was full of joy and enjoyment and the best jazz. Artists like Al Jolson, Louis Armstrong, and Duke Ellington. Yes, everything at this party was beautiful and fantastic, like a visit to his favorite era in a time machine. I wish time could stand still for me, then I wouldn't have to leave in a few hours and go back to reality.

***

"Look at Charles, I don't think anyone is having more fun at this party than him," Nadim said with a wink, indicating the tipsy physician, currently dancing with another doctor from the hospital. "By the way, did he tell you about the Porsche he got as a gift recently?"

"Porsche?" Murad repeated absently, preoccupied and not really paying attention to what Nadim was saying.

"The Porsche! An executive who had received a kidney transplant gave it to him."

"But Charles doesn't perform that kind of surgery. It's not his specialty." Murad interjected, unconvinced.

"I know, I know. But who said that Charles did the surgery? Did I say that?

"But you said…" Murad didn't finish what he was about to say, his attention captured by something on the balcony.

"You and I and everyone else at the hospital knows who performed the surgery. We know that Charles had nothing to do with the patient apart from his role as the department head where the surgery was performed. To the patient, the matter is subject, in the end, to the impression he gets – or, to put it plainly, by what he is told to believe. So, true enough, Charles did not perform the surgery, but as head of the surgery department, he manages every detail, overseeing the conduct of every operation, even when it isn't his specialty... that's the image Charles projects to everyone, thanks to Nasser Alquwit. So they both win: Charles gets a Porsche, and Nasser's reputation grows because he was the one who provided an international blue-eyed surgeon."

Nadim stopped talking when he noticed his friend had stopped listening, he looked out to the balcony to see what had seized Murad's attention.

"Sarah looks radiant tonight, doesn't she? You are a magician, Murad, not just a surgeon. She's a walking billboard for your skills." Nadim said, teasing Murad, who barely heard what his friend said. He wasn't really paying much attention to Sarah herself, either. Something else had captured his attention, something he wasn't anticipating, something he never thought he would see.

He doubted what he saw at first. *Impossible. There's no way it could be her.* His heart began to pound as he stared, *Could it be?* Only her profile was visible as she spoke to Sarah, and his doubt began to shift. Then she turned and he could see her face clearly. Every trace of doubt finally vanished, and he knew her as surely as he knew himself and the place he stood. *Hadeel!*

***

Murad started towards her unconsciously. He wanted to confront her, to ask her why she had done what she did. What made her testify against him? Why did she disavow him? Was she forced to? So many questions had haunted him and confounded him, and here was his chance to get his answers from Hadeel. *You have to tell me everything. Nothing less will do.*

"Ah, Murad. Good, you made it. Let me introduce you to…"

Sarah started to say when her lover approached, but Murad interrupted, "I know her quite well, and she knows me, too."

"Excuse me?" Hadeel said, clearly surprised, "have we met?"

The question hit Murad like a bolt from the blue. *The nerve! She denies knowing me!*

"I didn't know that a year would be enough time to forget the man you gave false testimony about! The man whose only sin was to think about marrying you one day!'

"Murad!" Sarah was mortified by what she saw unfolding. She looked around until she saw Nadim who immediately understood from her body language that something serious happened. He rushed over.

"Murad, there is clearly something wrong with you. There must be some misunderstanding. This is Dr. Hadeel, Mr. Wajih's wife."

"Now I get it!" Murad jumped in. "It was all a plot by Wajih! He had his sights set on you, despite having married your sister."

"Murad, please stop making a scene!" Sarah tried to say, horrified at her lover's outburst. She didn't know what to say or do to stem the flow of accusations. She could see from Hadeel's expression that she did not know Murad at all, so this was all coming from a complete stranger.

"Good evening everyone, is everything alright?" Nadim asked, but he could see that Murad was furious, their hostess was embarrassed and upset, and her friend was caught completely off-guard; things were not alright.

"Nadim, please allow me to introduce Hadeel. I've been telling you about her for a year now; ever since we bumped into each other in that café in Jeddah. She is the reason I came to Riyadh," Murad said flatly.

"Murad, what are you talking about? Are you alright? You look ill."

"Nadim, would you please take Murad to the guest room, he can rest there for a bit."

"I'm fine, I don't need to rest! Nadim, do you remember what I told you in Jeddah? How it made you sympathize with me, and got you to find me work at the Elsaaidi Hospital? If it weren't for what happened there, I would not be here!" Then Murad looked at Sarah, "And I would never have performed the surgeries for you that I have."

"Murad, please, just come with me…"

"No. I will not come with you. Not until you tell them what I spoke to you about in Jeddah."

"What are you talking about? I really don't know what you're referring to, the last time I saw you in Jeddah was years and years ago. Anyway, I didn't have anything to do with you coming to the Elsaaidi Hospital; you've been here almost three years."

What he heard stopped Murad in his tracks, for a moment he was dizzy and felt like he might lose his balance. To have Hadeel deny him, there was an explanation for that. But for his friend Nadim to deny having met with him in Jeddah a year ago along with everything they had spoken about there, that was something else entirely – and there was no way to explain it!

(11)
Mohamed? Mohamed!

It's crazy. **I'm** crazy – to think that I'm right and everyone else, everyone, is wrong. No, that can't be right. I must be the one who's got it wrong. The things in my memory, they aren't real. That's it. They were all surprised! There is no other reason they would be. I'm exhausted from overwork. That must be it. Yes. I've worked too much, and it has taken its toll on me. I've started imagining things that never happened and denying things that did. I need to get my memory back! I need to get myself back! I've got to get my life back!

On a bed in the guest wing where Sarah insisted Nadim take him to rest, Murad kept going over the same thoughts in his mind. Her regard for him was plain to see, as was her fear of what was happening to him; she made no effort to hide it. He was even starting to believe that their relationship, in her eyes at least, was more familiar than surgeon and patient, much more. Even so, even with the great affection she was showing towards him, Murad felt nothing for her. To him, she was just a patient he had operated on several times. *How did it come to this?* He tried again and again to remember something, anything, but it was futile.

"Sweetheart? Are you alright? You've really got me worried."

Lost in thought, Murad hadn't heard the door open and close.

"Mrs. Sarah." He said.

"Mrs. Sarah? What is with you? Why are you talking to me like that? We're the only ones here."

Murad didn't know how to respond. When he started to get out of bed, she got there first and cradled his head against her chest. "My dear, can you explain? I want to understand. Has someone upset you? Have I done something to upset you without knowing?"

"Please!" he said, trying to extract himself. "We're in your husband's house!"

"Since when has that bothered you? Why have you never said something before?"

Yet again, Murad was knocked back by surprise at what she said. *Before? When? What 'before' are you talking about?* Shaking his head, he said the only thing that came to mind, "This person... this man you are describing, it isn't me. It's not me!"

Instead of answering him, Sarah just sat staring into his eyes, full of her own surprise at first, but it quickly turned to anger when she started to suspect that Murad was trying to push her away, or to end their relationship. She stood quickly, saying nothing, turned her back on him and went through the door.

No sooner did Sarah leave then Nadim came in, also still bewildered by everything he had witnessed that night. The idea of Murad having an affair with Ghanim

Elsaaidi's wife had never occurred to him. What was even more perplexing was that, in the depth of her feelings for her lover, Sarah made no effort to hide it. It was as if she wanted him, and everyone else, to know!

"My God, what a night!" he said as he lowered himself to sit on the bed, looking at Murad, who still stood where he had after fleeing Sarah's embrace.

"It seems like there's a lot about you I didn't know. It's like Virginia says about you. Still waters run deep. It'd probably be best if you go on home once you've rested. I'll do my thing and try to smooth things over with Dr. Hadeel. I'm sure her husband won't be happy about what happened if she decides to tell him what you said. Not to mention, of course, what Nasser Elquwit will do. As for the other thing, we need to have a long talk about that."

"What other thing are you talking about?" Murad asked, though Nadim's answering sly smile gave him a hint.

"Alrighty. I'll leave you to rest a bit. I'll go and salvage what I can. Oh – by the way, that Tunisian waiter, I think his name is Mohamed? He wanted me to pass on his wishes that you'll feel better. He wanted to come in person to check on you, but I took care of it."

"The Tunisian waiter?" Murad said, surprised.

"You've seen him around. He's worried about you. He thinks you're friends."

As if he were taken aback, he asked "Mohamed what?" and looked at Nadim, who shook his head, signaling that he didn't understand the question.

"What is his family name? Mohamed what?" he asked again.

"I don't know what his last name is."

Murad didn't stick around to try to explain to Nadim why he was asking; he headed straight for the door without looking back to see Nadim's shock at his sudden, strange behavior.

***

The whole situation is just not right! There has been some kind of mistake. It's insane, but there's no arguing with the facts. Either the world has gone crazy, or I have. At first, he thought the problem was internal, but there was a small voice inside his head was trying to dissuade him. Murad was about to squash that voice, but he didn't; something made it louder instead – the headache, the overlapping memories, the things that had happened to him and around him... there was an answer to the puzzle. There had to be, though he didn't know what it could be. He needed to confirm something first. He needed to know the family name of that Tunisian waiter!

Following directions from the people he asked along the way, Murad headed to the outside servants' suite, where they told him he could find Mohamed. The urgency in his voice when he asked the chamberlain made the man suspicious of the young fellow he had brought on as extra help for the Eid party, based on a recommendation from Nasser Alquwit.

"Sir, is there anything I might be able to help you with in Mohamed's stead?"

Murad was on the verge of saying, "No, you can't help me." Instead of wasting time answering, he hurried off. He wanted to hear it directly from Mohamed. He wanted to be certain about something that was bothering him, something that he thought he might be starting to understand; with every passing second, Murad was becoming more certain that he wasn't the crazy one.

The servants' wing was on the east side of the palace grounds, set apart from the residential building back among the trees. He knocked on the door. After a moment, he knocked again. No one came. When Murad started to turn away to continue looking for the waiter elsewhere, he heard something inside. He opened the door and called out. The lights were off, as though no one was there. But he could hear a voice, more of a whisper, was coming from upstairs. Murad looked for a switch to turn on the lights before he went deeper into the room.

"Mohamed? Mohamed, it's me, Dr. Murad."

No one answered. The place was obviously empty. But what about the whispers coming from above? He decided to go up, just to have a look. The voice came from a room at the end of the hall, but when he got there, it suddenly fell silent.

"Excuse me, is anyone in there? I'm Dr. Murad, I'm looking for a waiter named Mohamed." Yet again, there was no answer, so he decided to open the door, to investigate the source of the whispers. It was dim inside the chamber; a little light from outside filtered in through the closed blinds on the window. *There doesn't seem to be anyone here. Maybe I imagined the whispers…*

Turning to leave, Murad caught a glimpse of something on the ground near the bed. At first, he couldn't make out what it was, but when he focused on it, he knew exactly what it was. He quickly sought out the light switch, feeling for it with his right hand on the wall by the door. It took him a few seconds, but he found what he was looking for and light flooded the room, making plain what was on the floor. He ran to Mohamed; the Tunisian waiter's body lay there dead, eyes closed. Murad did a quick examination; he saw no cause of death. It looked like it might have been a heart attack. The whispers suddenly arose again, but this time, they were coming from behind him. Just as he started to turn to see who was there, he felt a powerful blow to the back of his head, and everything went dark.

(12)
A Drop from Above

"**M**ost people don't pay attention to the little things, but that is where the secret lay. That's what makes it possible to break people up into two groups; a small faction that looks and sees, and the larger part that looks, but they see nothing but what they want to see. In the end, however, that's just how life is. There is no getting around having a special minority and a general majority."

Murad wasn't listening to what was being said to him, in fact, he paid almost no attention to the speaker at all. He was preoccupied with taking stock as he came back to consciousness. His head spun and his vision was just starting to clear. He tried to recall what had happened before he lost consciousness. There was a body. Mohamed, the Tunisian waiter. Then came a hard blow to the back of his head. He didn't feel anything between that moment and now as he started to regain consciousness. Then he heard someone talking. The voice was familiar, he had heard it before, and not long ago.

"Let me ask you a question. Think of this as the most important question you've ever been asked; your answer will set the course of the rest of your life."

"Virginia?"

The shock he felt when he identified the speaker was only intensified by where he was and the people around him. He was sitting on the roof of a skyscraper. From the buildings he could see, he deduced that he was on top of the Elsaaidi Tower. Virginia stood in front of him, surrounded by three muscular men dressed all in black — her personal bodyguard.

"What is the meaning of this? Why am I here?"

"Murad, for tonight, I'll be asking the questions. If you can answer them, I'll give you the chance to question me as much as you like. For now, I need your answer. The cat. Is it alive or dead?"

"What?" He asked.

Virginia walked approached him and gracefully knelt in front of the chair. She leaned in, her head nearly touching his, searching his eyes as she asked again in a whisper: "How did you manage it? I don't know... Frankly, Murad, I would much rather risk not knowing the answer to this conundrum than take the risk of leaving you alive."

The last word had barely left Virginia's lips before Murad found himself flying off the tower's roof. It only took a moment, as though the men had been waiting for a prearranged signal. He felt nothing but confusion for those few moments. What cat was she talking about? What had he done that Virginia didn't know about? These questions had only just started to take shape in his mind when they threw him off. *Why?* He didn't bother trying to work out the solution; his time was up. None of it mattered now. Hadeel, Sarah's relationship to him, the Tunisian waiter Mohamed, none of the events in the world around him. Only his plummet towards the unyielding ground below.

It is said that as death approaches, a person will see his life flash before his eyes in every detail, like a movie. In those moments, Murad saw more than just the years of his life. The film he saw passed in the blink of an eye. It still didn't matter, though. It would only be a few moments before it all ended anyway; the ground was approaching at an alarming rate. Less than a second... that was all he had left. His life would end in less than a second leaving him without an answer to the final question – Why?

It was a bare femtosecond (one thousand trillionth of a second) before he slammed into the pavement when everything puffed to smoke – as though nothing were real. From the void, he heard a familiar voice whisper, "Nothing will be that has not already been, nothing will end that has not already ended."

(13)
The Sultan's Oath

The prices of goods in Otrar, on the easternmost edge of the Khwarezmian Empire, a semi-autonomous kingdom under the Abbasid Caliphate, had doubled. A bag of rice cost a single dirham a month ago. Now the price had jumped up to three dirhams, and that only if you could find it. Grain merchants blamed the increase in the cost of rice to the small numbers of caravans coming from China and India as the Mongols increased their raids, burning crops and fallow land alike in the East. The general population, however, chalked it up to the greed of Yanal Khan, governor of Otrar, and brother of Turkan Khatoun, mother to the Sultan Alaa-Eddin Mohamed Khwarezmshah. He had increased taxes on the merchants, forcing them to increase their prices in order to recoup their losses. The root cause might even lie with the people themselves. The people who lived in Otrar had hated Yanal Khan from the first year of his rule; they even whispered about him behind closed doors, changing his title from Khan (leader) to Chok (little). When this nickname reached Yanal's ears, his rage pushed him to inflict even greater suffering on the citizens, making them hate him even more.

Many of Otrar's dignitaries tried to meet with Sultan Alaa-Eddin in order to ask him to remove Yanal. Everyone who went, though, ended up meeting with his vizier, Najm-Eddin Kablak. He always made vast promises but never produced anything. The dignitaries despaired, particularly when they realized that neither the Vizier nor the Sultan himself could remove Yanal Chok without the approval of Turkan Khatoun. The Sultan could not go against his mother's orders; she had too much influence in the Empire; a full third of the army were members of her tribe and would take no orders unless they came from her or someone she had empowered.

Everyone knew of Turkan Khatoun's power and how she dominated her son, the Sultan. She even made him follow through on the oath he made concerning his second wife, Nouran Khatoun, mother to his eldest son, Jalal-Eddin Manguberdi. In a rage, he had vowed she would spend three nights outside his territory.

***

The hatred the people of the Empire of Khwarezm harbored for Sultan Alaa-Eddin Mohamed and his mother Turkan Khatoun was matched only by their love for Nouran Khatoun and her son Jalal-Eddin. Not only did Nouran hail from one of the best-regarded Turkic tribes, she was the only daughter of the Qadi of Bukhara, Abu Abdullah Mohamed bin Bushtaq Al-Nishapuri.

Her father had died some twenty-five years before these events, and stories of his rich life experiences had spread throughout Bukhara and the rest of the cities of the Empire of Khwarezm. Bukhara had never had a Qadi who matched his sense of fairness, integrity, and compassion. Moreover, he was never stingy with either wisdom or money. He died poor, leaving no inheritance for his daughter Nouran other than knowledge and good morals.

In her youth, Nouran was one of Bukhara's great beauties, her beauty only surpassed by her gentle demeanor. She had been very close to her father and learned much under his tutelage before he died. His death was a tragedy for all the people of Bukhara. When Alaa-Eddin was just the Emir of Bukhara, while his father was still Sultan, his first wife had failed to provide him with a male heir, so he started looking for a second wife. The people close to him suggested Nouran, the best of the ladies in Bukhara. When Qadi Abu Abdullah Mohamed bin Bushtaq Al-Nishapuri died, their great love for the qadi transferred to his daughter.

Turkan Khatoun despised the girl every bit as much as the people loved her. She hated Nouran so much, in fact, that she tried to convince her son, the Sultan, not to make Jalal-Eddin heir to the throne, holding out hope that his first wife, Qatr-Elnada, would bear him a son who would follow his father instead of Nouran's son. Turkan's wish was partially granted; Qatr-Elnada had a son, Ghiyath-Eddin, several years after Jalal-Eddin was born. Ghiyath-Eddin was the Sultan's second son and held Turkan's favor – not for his knowledge or laudable behavior, or even for his talent in combat. None of these things made him better his elder brother; all she cared about was that he was not the child of Nouran, daughter of Abu Abdullah Mohamed bin Bushtaq Al-Nashapuri.

***

Otrar was the final stop for Emir Jalal-Eddin Manguberdi's caravan before it left the boundaries of the Khwarezmian Empire. His mother, Nouran Khatoun, was in the caravan; they were on their way to spend three nights outside the holdings of Sultan Alaa-Eddin Mohamed, in order to fulfill the Sultan's oath, made in a rage on the day he returned to Bukhara. His raid on the piece of Iraq still ruled by Abbasid Caliph Annasser Li-Dinillah Ahmed Bin Al-Hasan had been a failure. The plan had been to move on to Baghdad after the raid and to try and bring down the city and add it and its territory to his empire. Then he would announce the fall of the Abbasid Caliphate and appoint whoever he wanted to as a new Caliph for the Muslims. But the Caliph's armies were able to force him to retreat to his own territory where he could plan for another attempt next year after recovering. The Sultan's daughter, Fayrouz, and her husband, the cavalry commander Mamdoud Elkhwarezmi, both fell during the campaign.

"You caused her death! I told you again and again that Allah would not be with you in the campaign you launched against the Muslims in Iraq!" Nouran screamed at the Sultan when she received news of the death of her youngest daughter and son-in-law.

"Come now! Have you lost your mind? To speak to the Sultan so!" Turkan Khatoun, also at the council, raged.

"It is Allah's punishment! It is Allah's punishment!" Nouran continued, weeping.

Sultan Alaa-Eddin replied, "Calm down! Your pain is my pain, only my pain is the greater. You have lost a daughter; I have lost a daughter, and several of the best commanders in my armies."

"Damn you and your armies! Killing Muslims instead of killing Allah's enemies!"

"The Abbasids *are* Allah's enemies! Their corruption has spread through every level of society. I swear to Allah; their evil is greater than the Westerners! Weren't you with me when we heard the Fatwa of the High Qadi Abu Abdel-Aziz Yahya bin Rihan that declared the Abbasid Caliphate were unbelievers because they had transgressed the boundaries set by Allah by permitting the sale of intoxicants in the markets of Baghdad and by their silence about the heretics; the one concerning lost souls spreading poison in the ears of the people, tempting them away from their faith?"

"You and your High Qadi can go to hell!" Nouran raged, inches from her husband's furious face.

"I swear, if you don't stop this screaming..."

"What will you do, oh great Sultan? What more can you to do me, oh murderer of my daughter?!"

The Sultan couldn't control himself, particularly with his wife screaming at him in front of his mother who clearly disapproved of what was happening. It was then that he uttered the oath that forced Nouran Khatoun to go to Otrar, to rest and resupply before leaving the Empire's lands for the territory of the Mongols, where they would spend three days outside the holdings of Sultan Alaa-Eddin Mohamed Khwarezmshah as punishment for her insolence.

(14)
The Journey Begins

Everything around him had changed. *Where did the buildings go? Where's Virginia, where are her guards?* There was nothing but green plains as far as he could see, ending in mountains along the horizon. *How did this happen? Am I dead or dreaming?* Murad kept searching with his eyes, examining his surroundings, completely perplexed as he searched for anything that might provide an explanation for what had happened. There was nothing around him but green earth, blue sky, and a cold breeze easterly wind. *How did I get here?* Trying to assess every possibility was driving him crazy. Nothing he thought of could explain what had happened. The desire to scream as loud as he could possessed him for a moment, but his voice betrayed him. His throat was so constricted with fear, nothing could get past it. Suddenly, as he stood in confused anticipation, he heard howling nearby. *Wolves!*

"Don't be afraid. They can't hurt you. They are more afraid of you than you are of them. Wolves have excellent senses; they can detect things that can't be seen with the naked eye."

Murad spun quickly, he had been looking in the direction the voice came from only a moment before and saw no one. It was like the speaker had sprouted suddenly from under the ground!

The man approached. Murad was taken aback by his clothing; he looked like he had stepped out of a historical series on television, like the ones that satellite channels broadcast during Ramadan each year. His clothing consisted of a pair of trousers under a white shirt that extended just below his knees. A black cloak rested on his shoulders and he had a green turban on his head. He was studying Murad very closely, like a scientist with a slide under a microscope.

"Please help me. I don't know how I got here. Where am I? Who are you? What happened? This is insane! Insane! No, it's a dream! It must be, it can't be anything else. No, a nightmare! Please, help me wake up!" Murad cried, beginning to babble the same questions over and over. The man watched him without interrupting, leaving Murad to wear himself down. Only when Murad stopped did he speak in a calm voice:

"Life and death. Slumber and wakefulness. Dream and reality. Green land and devastation. The past and the future. Opposites. But closer to one another than most people can imagine. I cannot answer most of the questions you ask now, but I can answer your questions about where you find yourself. You are two hundred miles southeast of the city of Otrar."

Murad was shaken by his words, then started to look around again. "Otrar? Is this a city in the Jazan region? Who brought me here?"

"No, it is a long way from the Arabian Peninsula, as are you."

"A long way? How did I get here? Are you with Virginia?"

The man gave no response, he simply stared. Murad, who had calmed a little before hearing the first answer, immediately spun back up into a frenzy. His emotions swung between control and panic like a pendulum; he couldn't settle himself.

"Why don't you answer me? There must be some kind of conspiracy! Yeah, that's it. There is a conspiracy! But… I don't know what it is after." He stopped talking when he remembered that he had been thrown from the roof of the Elsaaidi Tower and what had happened in the instant before he hit the ground.

"People often ask questions that are impossible to answer simply because they were asked at the wrong time or in the wrong situation. In doing so, they often ignore the most important questions, thinking they already know the answers; meanwhile, the answer they actually need is the furthest thing from their imagination. It would be better for you, stranger, to ask yourself who you are."

That last sentence made Murad stop. "I'm Muard Qutuz, cosmetic surgeon…." His voice faded as he spoke, and he didn't finish his statement. Instead, he started to question himself. *But which Murad am I? The one I think I am? Or the one everyone around me thinks I am?* Then he looked at the man in his odd garb, *Is this character for real, or is he just a lunatic spouting nonsense? Or maybe, for some reason, he wants me to doubt myself.*

Questions started spinning around in his head, leaving him dizzy. Am I really asking the wrong thing, ignoring the critical issue at the root of it all? Do I really not know myself, the self I've lived with all these years? If I don't know who I am, what **do** I know? No. Impossible. I am Murad Qutuz, cosmetic surgeon. I am sane. The world around me is crazy. I'm right. The people around me have lost their minds. I know myself perfectly. Yes. I know myself. I'm not the problem! He reassured himself, hoping to convince himself of what he had begun, deep inside, to doubt.

(15)

The Convoy from the Great Khan

The warrior on horseback intercepted of the convoy of the Great Mongol Khan to the Khwarzemian Empire at a full gallop. The convoy had set up camp the night before, three days from the city of Otrar, its first stop on the road to the great city of Bukhara, where Sultan Alaa-Eddin Khwarzemshah lived.

The warrior made his way to the caravan commander, Tenukei, and reported what he saw on his secret scouting mission.

"Commander. I found him. He isn't far from here."

Tenukei smiled. He had known the horseman would find him where Tabtinkar said he would be. "The great shaman is never wrong."

"but..." the warrior continued then hesitated.

"But what?" Tenukei asked firmly.

"He was alone. There was no one with him."

Tenukei was surprised by what he heard. "But Tabtinkar spoke of two men, not one!"

"Yes, commander. But it is as I reported. A man of average height, strong build, round face, and a thick black beard. He wore a green turban. Exactly as described, but the other man wasn't there."

The scout described the man just as Tabtinkar had. *But where is the other man?* Tenukei knew that killing one man would do no good. They must both die together. That was the order from Tabtinkar. If the man with the green turban was the only one to appear, it would have to wait until his companion showed up. There would be no way of identifying the second man otherwise. The shaman had been unable to describe him and had given no clear reason why.

The whole thing seemed off to Tenukei. If he didn't know Tabtinkar's powers as well as he did, and the horrors Tabtinkar could create, he would never have agreed to this mission; a secret kept from the merchants in the caravan as well as Princess Yasimi, Genghis Khan's granddaughter, who was accompanying the caravan.

Tenukei knew that he had to go there and see this man for himself. There was no room for error. Tabtinkar made it clear that the future of the Mongols hinged on this move.

(16)
Bodiless

So many unanswered questions. It wasn't just about what had been happening to him right this moment, it was also about what had been happening to him and the world around him for some time now – and there was no way to tell how long it had been going on. It was even possible that whatever was happening had nothing to do with Murad's main question – *Who am I?* That was nothing but a pointless philosophical question serving to distract him from more important things. Murad still believed that if he could just figure out what was behind all of this, everything else would fall into place.

He had hardly noticed much of what had happened to him, but now it seemed as though some of those details were critical pieces of the puzzle. But how? He knew that the answer wouldn't help him while he was in this unfamiliar place, brought here by inexplicable means, for incomprehensible reasons. One thing he did know, however, was that Virginia was the key to finding the answer; she was the last one he saw before appearing here. The only sensible course of action he could come up with was to return to Riyadh, tell Nadim Alzoud everything and ask him for advice. *I doubt he'll believe a word I say, particularly after the party. But I don't have anywhere else to turn now. I have to get back to Riyadh. Then we'll see. There must be an explanation."*

"Pardon me, friend." Murad called out to the man who had spent the last few minutes searching the northern horizon as though expecting someone to come.

The man turned towards him, then approached. "Abdel-Rahman, you can use that name."

"And I am Murad. Please, Mr. Abdel-Rahman. Do you have any means of transportation that could get me to the city you said is about two hundred miles from here?

"Otrar."

"Right, Otrar. Is there an airport there?"

Abel Rahman smiled instead of answering. His silence was perplexing, and Murad was starting to suspect he was a simple villager.

"Mr. Abdel-Rahman, could you give me directions to the nearest highway so I can find a car to take me to Otrar? The sun's about to set, and I don't think it's wise to be out in the open like this."

"Don't be afraid, we won't stay out here long. We'll be joining a caravan on its way to Otrar."

"A caravan? You mean Bedouins will be going by? Ohhh…" the man's strange attire finally made sense. *He must be part of this Bedouin caravan. Maybe he wandered away when he saw me.*

"Here they come."

When Murad followed the man's gaze, he could see several men on horseback approaching swiftly from the horizon. They seemed to be racing the wind. For just a moment, Murad felt comforted by their approach, but that quickly faded as they got close enough for him to see them clearly.

***

"Greetings in the name of the Lord of the Blue Sky." Tenukei said to the man who exactly matched the description provided by Tabtinkar.

"Greetings in the name of the God of the Universe." Answered Abdel-Rahman.

Tenukei looked around, but there was no sign of a second man.

"Are you alone here?"

"Do you see anyone here other than myself and your party?" Abdel-Rahman answered, now surrounded by four Mongol horsemen.

"What are you doing in the wilderness all alone? Aren't you afraid wolves will attack you?"

"The wolves don't scare me, horseman."

"What does scare you, then? Us?" Tenukei asked with a mocking toss of his head, bringing soft laughter from his men.

"I only fear the Creator who made me, you, and the wolves."

Tenukei was not surprised to hear this response. He just wanted to draw his sword and put an end to this. But Tabtinkar had been clear in his instructions. *You must kill both men.* But there was only one man here, where was the second? Tenukei thought a moment about what he

101

should do next, then decided he didn't have any other choice.

"I'm Tenukei, commander of the caravan bringing Princess Yasimi, granddaughter of the King of all Kings of the world, Genghis Khan, to Otrar. From there, we will be going on to Bukhara. If you are traveling in the same direction, you are welcome to join us."

Tenukei saw only two paths forward at this point: either the man would accept the invitation to accompany them, thus buying the commander time to report to Tabtinkar and get new instructions, or he would kill the man here and now if he refused. *One man is better than none,* he thought.

"Thank you, Tenukei, for your magnanimity. I have no objection to joining you." Abdel-Rahman said, having gotten what he wanted.

***

Murad couldn't understand what had just happened. Genghis Khan? The Mongols? Impossible! Why can't they see me? Where am I? What kind of nightmare is this?! This is insane!

"You lot! Why don't you see me? Why can't you hear me?!" he shouted at the Mongol horsemen. It was no good; as far as they were concerned, he didn't exist. Then he thought of something and looked at himself. He discovered the worst part of the whole situation since he appeared in this plain surrounded by mountains.

"Where are my hands? Where are my feet? Where's my body?!?" For the first time since he was thrown from the skyscraper, since he appeared in this strange place and – so it seemed – ancient time, he realized that he had no body!

(17)

In Waiting

Emir Jalal-Eddin Manguberdi found his mother Nouran Khatoun where he expected, she always spent time with her grandson, Mahmoud bin Mamdoud after the dawn prayer. Young Mahmoud was twelve years old and was working on completing his memorization of the Qur'an. Nouran was correcting his Tajweed and, at the same time, explaining the meaning of the verses that puzzled him. This had been the job of Fairouz, his mother, who had first learned from her mother. When Nouran learned that her daughter had been killed accompanying her husband on the Sultan's raid, she decided she would play the role of tutor rather than see her grandson sent to Damascus to learn from Syria's scholars. She didn't want her grandson to grow up to be a killer like his father; she wanted to see him become a respected scholar like her own father, Qadi Mohamed bin Bushtaq Al-Nishapuri. To that end, she always kept him close to herself and as far as possible from her husband the Sultan. She even kept him away from her own son, Jalal-Eddin, who was a cavalryman and soldier himself. Nouran had no desire to lose her grandson to the same fate.

"May Allah grant you a fine morning, mother."

"And you, my son. Will we be leaving Otrar today?"

"Tomorrow, if Allah wills. We are still waiting for the warriors we sent to scout ahead to return. We will be crossing land that has been taken by the Mongols. We must be cautious."

"And what could those savages do to us? A single Khwarezmian warrior could easily handle a hundred of them!" Mahmoud interjected with fierce pride.

"Especially if that Khwarezmian warrior was you." Jalal-Eddin teased his nephew.

"Leave Mahmoud alone, Jalal-Eddin. His future lies with study and scholars, not warriors and battlefields."

"Mother, we are kings and emirs of this land. The people expect us to protect them and bring them the spoils of war. There are plenty of men to tend to scholarship, and Allah has put them at our service. We shelter them, and we will not shirk our duty. But why should we do their job? I swear, if we do their job, they will want to do ours."

"That's your father talking." She answered. "Is this how I raised you? What can I say other than that Allah shall judge me. I hope to find in Mahmoud what I lost in you." Shaking her head, Nouran's displeasure was clear.

"I swear, mother, you'll find I do nothing that does not fill your heart with joy. If I am a just Sultan, I will be the more so thanks to the scholars and their knowledge."

She cut him off, saying "Provided your father designates you his heir."

Surprised, he answered, "And why would he not? I am his eldest son."

"Because Turkan does not want Nouran's son to become Sultan. She wants her younger grandson, Ghiyath-Eddin, son of her daughter-in-law Qatr-Elnada. Your father doesn't dare go against her orders."

"Mother, you shouldn't think so poorly of Grandmother Turkan. I am blood of her blood, descended from her just as much as Ghiyath-Eddin is. She would not violate tradition so much as to put the younger brother before the elder."

"My son, your problem is that you trust people too much. The thing I fear most is that one day you will place your trust in someone who doesn't deserve it, and it will result in your downfall." Nouran was quiet for a few moments, giving her son the chance to think about what she said. Then she went on, "Did you not notice how we were received in Otrar yesterday? Is that how a future Sultan would be received?"

"What of our welcome at the city gates? The people were all but lifted and carried our horses with us still mounted in their joy at our approach!" he answered.

"Do not judge only by what you see. That which you do not see reveals the truth."

"What might it be that I did not see, mother?"

"The governor of Otrar. Turkan Khatoun's brother."

(18)
The Great Khan's Granddaughter

Temujin and Borte's love for their granddaughter Yasimi was equaled only by Tabtinkar's obsession and loathing. Some thought this was because she was the daughter of Jochi, Temujin's eldest son, born to Borte shortly after her capture by Chiledu Khan of the Merkit. Some, including Tabtinkar, believed that Jochi was not actually Temujin's son, and that the Great Khan had claimed him as his own in order to cover the shame of his beloved wife, Borte. His love for her was held up as an example far and wide. That's why Tabtinkar knew that Temujin would love Jochi even if he were not Temujin's own, simply because he was part of Borte, even if the other part of the child came from Temujin's enemy Chiledu.

Temujin reacted harshly anytime anyone cast doubt on Jochi's parentage. He even beheaded one of his own generals on the very day he heard him call Jochi a Merkit. In doing so, he ensured no one, not even members of his family, would question Jochi's parentage. That might be the reason why Yasimi was the focus of so much of Temujin and Borte's care, though no such warmth was forthcoming from the great Shaman Tabtinkar. Not only was Yasimi the most beautiful of Temujin's granddaughters, she was also the cleverest and bravest of them. People often described her as taking closely after her grandmother with some of the Great Khan's wisdom and cleverness mixed in.

Her courage sprang from her great curiosity, which led her one day to try something no one else had dared. She entered Tabtinkar's tent where he was on one of his spiritual journeys. She wanted to see what the Shaman was doing when he secreted himself away for days at a time. He was terrifying that day. No one had heard anyone shout like he did; it sounded like a peal of thunder in a stormy sky. Everyone thought that Tabtinkar would curse Yasimi, whose face was pale, either from terror at what she had seen in the Shaman's tent or from the furious shout. If it weren't for Borte coming at the nick of time, Tabtinkar's curse surely would have fallen upon the girl, not yet nine years old. Yasimi never told what she had seen in the Shaman's tent, and no one who knew her dared ask; everyone knew better than to pry into Tabtinkar's secrets without his permission. To do so was to violate the greatest of taboos and would result in swift retribution both in this world and the spirit world. This meant that Yasimi bore a stigma from that day on among most of the Mongols, even if no one dared say anything aloud in fear of how Genghis Khan would react. The result was that Yasimi was raised apart from the other children, giving her grandparents the opportunity to dote on her in a way they could not with the rest of their grandchildren. It is also why Genghis Khan entrusted her education to those of his advisors who did not believe in the shamanism as most Mongols did; they did not fear the wrath of the Great Shaman Tabtinkar. These advisors were Muslims, Christians, and Manicheans who had found their way to the seat of the Mongol Khan where the doors stood open to all who would acknowledge and submit to him as King of Kings on this Earth. Despite the way her grandparents doted on her, and despite her beauty, courage, and unique intelligence, Yasimi, was not desired by any of the Mongol men when she blossomed into womanhood. Not only was she the child of Jochi, whose parentage was in doubt, she was worse – she was the girl who nearly brought down the curse of the Great Shaman Tabtinkar.

***

Yasimi approached the man who had just joined their caravan, who she assumed, based on his dress, was from a Muslim land. She was terribly bored and wanted to talk to someone other than those who had been by her side for the months-long journey that set out from Karakorum, the Mongol capital city. She considered the man for a time before opening a dialogue.

"I am Yasimi, daughter of Jochi, son of the King of Kings of the Earth, Genghis Khan." She said, making no attempt to hide her pride. "Who are you, stranger?"

"Abdel-Rahman." The man replied.

"You are not a native of this country. You appear to be an Arab."

"How do you know this?"

"Your pale, reddish skin. Your long nose. The arch of your brows. All of these are common among Arabs. But your face is round, so it appears that one of your ancestors must have married a Turk."

Abdel-Rahman looked at the young lady before answering. "Your ability to speak the tongue of the Arabs is only surpassed by your insight. You have done well in your studies."

Yasimi smiled at the compliment from the man. Based on how little he said, though, she feared he might not have enough knowledge or intelligence for it to be worth continuing the conversation. *Just an Arab, up from the Arabian Peninsula seeking wealth in the lands beyond the river.*

She was about to spur her horse onward to the head of the caravan when Abdel-Rahman made an observation of his own. "My guess is that your teacher must have been Rustam bin Yazdashir, the Manichean. He did well in teaching you about the Arabs and their language, but not so well in initiating you into his dualist faith."

Yasimi was astounded by this profound insight; she examined him more closely, then asked in a shocked tone, "How could you know this?"

Abdel-Rahman gestured towards a small medallion she wore around her neck, half black, half white. "I met Rustam long ago in Baghdad, before he came to your lands to escape the confines of Muslim lands. I heard that Genghis Khan honored him for his knowledge, though Rustam did not convince the Khan of his faith. It appears as though he succeeded with you where he failed with your grandfather."

Yasimi grew angry at this, feeling that he was testing her. "I am no gullible child, believing everything anyone tells me."

"Yet you believed in the teachings of Mani, shared with you by Rustam."

"What is wrong with Mani's teachings? Does he not appeal to goodness and renounce evil?" Yasimi answered hotly.

"Enjoining the good and renouncing all evil, this is well. But the idea that there are two gods, a god of light from whom all good things emanate, and a god of darkness who is the source of all evil... that is the repugnant part."

"Repugnant!" Yasimi shouted at him, "What do you know of repugnant? You don't see what is repugnant! You do not see evil though it wraps you in darkness in order to hide its own repugnant face!"

Abdel-Rahman looked into her eyes as though he had been waiting for just this reaction, then asked, "And have you seen the evil as it surrounds you in darkness?"

Yasimi didn't respond. She wanted to tell him yes, I have seen what no one before me has. I have seen what must not be seen, when I entered the tent of the Shaman Tabtinkar. Now that I have grown, I pay the price. *Even the descendant of Genghis Khan cannot stand before the god of Darkness when he bares his fangs!* She wanted to tell him how she would never again see her parents, her brothers, he grandparents, or anyone else she loved or who loved her. *The god of darkness, about whom you know nothing, is behind it all!* Instead, she simply said:

"There are things that few people know."

"Very true. There are many things that many people do not know. I may be counted among them. Will you permit me a question, to help me find my way?"

Yasimi just nodded.

"Lying is a bad thing, is it not? In your belief system, who brought lies into the world, the god of light, or the god of darkness?

"It was the god of darkness, naturally."

"Naturally. Let us take a man who has repented from telling lies, so he says: 'I used to lie, now I have stopped.' Who is the source of this statement, the god of light or the god of darkness?"

"The god of light, of course."

"But according to the teachings of Manichaeism, the god of light is not the source of lies. So how could the man say he lied when it was the god of darkness who lied? If the source of this statement was the god of darkness, then he speaks true - but how could he do such a thing, when it is he from whom no truth comes?"

Yasimi was confounded by the puzzle in which she found her mind enmeshed. She tried to find a way out of the conundrum but could not. She tried to remember everything Rustam bin Yazdashir taught her. *Surely Rustam had faced such a question before. He had to have.* But... but her memory availed her nothing. Her mind was frozen by the query. *Damn you, stranger! You have not seen what I have seen. If that was not the god of darkness, then who was it?*

While trying to work out the puzzle set by Abdel-Rahman, Yasimi heard a sound like a thunderclap from the front of the caravan followed by cries and chaos.

"Your highness! Princess! Your highness!" a warrior cried, driving his horse towards Yasimi as though there were a dragon on his tail.

"What is it, Akwadi? What is all the screaming about?" She asked the clearly frightened warrior.

"Tenukei, your highness. Tenukei!" he panted.

"What about Commander Tenukei? Did something happen to him?"

"He fell from his horse and was dead when he hit the ground!"

"He just fell down dead? How? How could such a thing happen to a strong, healthy warrior like Tenukei?"

Akwadi hesitated, not knowing how to answer his princess. How could he explain to her what happened? The commander chatting easily with him like usual and then, with no warning, he stiffened, putting his hand on his chest as though something had struck him in the heart, yet there was no sign of injury.

(19)

Dichotomies

L ife. Death. These two words no longer held any meaning. Which state was he in? Was he dead or alive? Or was he in some other state that he'd never learned the name of? Murad tried to come up with answers to his own questions, but he couldn't. How could a person answer a question on a subject they knew nothing about? When they'd never seen or heard of anything remotely like it? No less strange than everything else was that, for some unknown reason, this odd man, Abdel-Rahman, was the only one who could see him. Stranger still, Abdel-Rahman was not surprised at all. He simply took it in stride like it was an everyday thing for him. *And he still didn't try to help me. He didn't try to explain anything to me*. What happened, happened. *Why didn't he answer my questions?*

"Am I alive or dead? If this is death, tell me so I can rest!" he shouted at Abdel-Rahman, then collapsed in a fit of laughter when he heard his own words. The laughter covered his deep anxiety, sadness, and helplessness. *If this is death, tell me so I can rest … has death become a respite for me now?*

But Abdel-Rahman never gave him a clear answer, not one that satisfied him at any rate. The man spoke in riddles that left Murad more lost than he had been.

"If you want to live, then you are alive. If you want to die, then you are dead." He said.

Murad shouted, "What rational human being would want to die?"

"Are all human beings rational?"

And so on. Every answer from Abdel-Rahman added to Murad's confusion.

"Why don't you give me a straight answer? Why don't you just tell me about what's happened to me?"

"Because you are the only person who can answer those questions. Why don't you try stopping all this complaining and try to see the reality around you?"

"Who said I haven't? I've tried, but it's no use!"

"You looked. You did not try to see. There is a big difference between looking and seeing."

Looking? Seeing? "What's the difference?" Murad wanted to ask, but he didn't. He knew that if he posed the question, the only answer he would get would be even more confusing. Hopeless, alone, and miserable, he didn't want to think or talk or even walk with the caravan anymore. That thought brought something to his attention he hadn't noticed before. Despite his lack of desire to walk, he was traveling with the caravan without physically moving. Not only that, but what he saw was something like watching a movie where the rules of time and space didn't apply; he could see things from more than one angle and from different points of view, though he didn't know how. More than that: he could observe events happening simultaneously as well as sequentially, which made things even worse. Strangest of all, he had somehow grown accustomed to this pluralistic view of events over time. He started to wonder then: was he the one controlling the shifts between events and different aspects of them, or was he seeing something that someone else wanted him to see. If it wasn't him, who was in control? Did this Abdel-Rahman have a hand in the matter? Stopping there, he began again from the beginning. *I'm sure Abdel-Rahman knows all the answers, but for some reason he doesn't want to tell me. Why is he treating me this way? Why?* Just as he started to circle around to the beginning again in a manic state, he heard a sound like thunder from the front of the caravan, and at the same time saw something like a shadow flit by, but it moved without a body. It was passing through the caravan, but none of the Mongols saw it or reacted to its presence. This shade appeared at the front of the caravan at the exact moment that Murad heard the shout, then it quickly vanished – but before it did, something strange happened. The spectral creature looked directly at Murad with a featureless face that seemed somehow familiar to him, then it smiled as it reached out to touch the caravan commander's chest with an arm made of black smoke.

***

Panic overcame the caravan as the news of Tenukei's death spread. The warriors guarding the caravan started asking each other how something like this could have happened with no warning. They even began to wonder if their commander had been under a curse of some kind.

"Was he complaining of any symptoms?" asked the senior merchant, Mohamed bin Ishaq Elbukhari, taking control of the situation in order to calm the members of the caravan, which was on the verge of chaos.

"No. He was talking to us like always. He did not show any signs of trouble." Several of the warriors responded.

"Alright. What happened, happened. There is no power greater than death; it can come as a surprise to anyone at any time. You must pull yourselves together and select a new commander to lead the caravan so we can get back on our way smoothly. Keep in mind that this caravan is carrying something more precious than the fine goods in our packs. The granddaughter of Genghis Khan is here!"

***

"I saw what happened!" Murad shouted, addressing Abdel-Rahman who appeared calm amid the chaos, as though he cared nothing for what had just transpired, or maybe he didn't know. "I don't get it, how did no one see it but me?"

"No one saw it, just as they do not see you." He answered evenly.

"What about you? Did you see that thing like I did?" Murad wanted to know.

"I saw it, just as I see you now." Abdel-Rahman told him with no indication that this was out of the ordinary

117

for him; as easily as he would speak of seeing a bird in the sky, which only increased Murad's awe of the man.

"Is this something normal? Doesn't it frighten you?"

"No."

"No?!" Murad cried out, "What's the 'no' answering? Not a normal thing? Or that it doesn't frighten you?"

"Both."

This unexpected and terse answer gave Murad pause. "Is that all you are going to say?"

"I would say so. You asked. I answered."

"Then answer this: what did we see?"

"Your question carries a strange contradiction."

"What?" Murad asked incredulously.

"You claim that you saw something. Then you ask me what you saw. You didn't see anything. You *looked* at its face, but you did not *see* anything, even if you think you did."

"I've had enough of your riddles!" Murad shouted at the top of his lungs in a fury. He was sure that if his voice was audible, everyone in the caravan would have heard him. "Why won't you give me a straight answer? Why won't you teach me, so I can understand what is happening around me? It's like you enjoy my ignorance!"

Abdel-Rahman didn't answer right away, instead giving Murad time to quiet down. Then he looked at Murad and said, "When the student is ready, the teacher will appear."

(20)
Disrupted Pleasure

Following his evening routine, Yanal Khan descended to his private chambers in the Spring Palace with his female servants, listening as one sang sweetly accompanied by an oud while he watched another slide into a sensual dance, pleasing to the eye, as the fingers of others rubbed scented oils from India and Sindh into his corpulent flesh. He was getting ready to choose one of the girls to spend the rest of the night with him in his bed, when his vizier, Khalid bin Mansour, asked permission to speak to him on an urgent matter that could not wait until morning. The governor detested this unwanted intrusion on his precious time. To him, there was nothing that could not be postponed, especially when it interrupted the idle chatter that was helping relieve the stress of the day; the eternal obligations of ruling and listening to the complaints the people.

"My lord, I'm sorry to bother you, but something important has come up."

"What could be so important that it cannot wait until tomorrow?" The governor asked sharply, his tone clearly agitated by the disruption of his private time with his concubines.

"I just received word that the advance warriors sent by Emir Jalal-Eddin have returned after seeing a caravan approaching Otrar, sent to us by the Mongol Khan."

Displeasure in his eyes, Yanal Khan gazed at his minister; the news was both unwelcome and unworthy of the interruption. "Really? You disturb me for this?"

"My lord, this is the first caravan to come to the Khwarezmian Empire since..."

"Hold on a second. When did the barbarian khanates unite enough that they could send us caravans?" the governor asked, cutting off his minister.

"My apologies, my lord, but several months ago I informed you that the Tatar tribes had unified, including the Merkit, the Niman, and some Turk tribes from the eastern steppes. They are all under the Mongol banner now, led by a man they call Genghis Khan."

"Alright, yes. I remember you saying something of the sort. What could they be carrying? The Mongol territory is a barren wasteland, there is nothing good there."

"My lord, the Mongols have taken over the kingdom of northern China. Genghis Khan controls the Silk Road."

"North China!" He cried. "How did the barbarians accomplish such a feat? Praise be to Allah who deposes kings at will! Do you think the caravan carries silk and other Chinese goods?" the governor practically salivated at the thought.

"Yes, my lord. And something even more important."

"What could possibly be more important than Chinese silk?"

"The Khan's granddaughter, and their highest merchant carries a letter for Sultan Alaa-Eddin."

(21)

Message for the
Sultan's Son

The residents of Otrar had never seen a caravan like the one that arrived that morning. An unending chain of camels, each bearing a different load; rice, beans, spices, rolls of silk and the finest wool. It looked like the Mongols had sent everything they owned on camelback to the Khwarezmian Empire. It wasn't just the size of the caravan that amazed the people; they were selling their goods at very low prices! Goods that Otrar's merchants would have sold for two or three dirhams were available now from the Mongols for one! Once word spread throughout the city, people flocked to the caravan in such numbers they had to erect barricades to control the flow of excited buyers.

The day after they arrived in Otrar, Mohamed bin Ishaq Elbukhari was permitted to appear before the governor who was surprised to see a Muslim from Bukhara leading a Mongol caravan.

"If my lord governor would permit me, I will share with him the story of how I came to be in this place."

Yanal Khan waved for the Sheikh to go on.

"Yes, my lord. I was born and raised in the great city of Bukhara, which has no peer in any land. Allah alone knows how much I desire to see her again after this long

122

absence which carried me from country to country and showed me the conditions of Allah's servants, and how Allah is able to elevate the weak and destitute, and to humiliate the great and mighty. My lord, I have seen great kings destroyed at the hands of those thought incapable of taking over a small village, to say nothing of taking over cities defended by great walls!

"My journey, my lord, began when I lost my way after my father died in Bukhara. I was not yet twenty years old. My mother was beautiful, and still in her youth when my father passed. Many offers came before she finally agreed to marry a man who seemed to be righteous. It quickly became obvious to me that this was a façade, hiding his true dark nature. He did wrong by me. He stole what my father had left for us. I complained about him to the man who was Qadi at that time, Mohamed bin Bushtaq Al-Nishapuri, may Allah have mercy on him, whose fairness and faith were renowned. However, my lord, it was as though the fates had different designs than this humble servant; the just Qadi died before he was able to examine my case. Another Qadi came. The latter was nothing like the former. He ruled in favor of my mother's husband – and I learned later that he had taken a bribe to pronounce this unjust ruling. Would that the situation had ended there, but no. After the ruling, I found myself homeless, expelled from my father's house when my mother was forced to choose between her vile husband and her son. May Allah forgive her and grant her clemency for this deed; she gave in to her husband though it meant she was done with me.

"This was very hard on me, my lord. I could not stay in Bukhara. There was nothing for me but to wander Allah's wide world seeking my way. I freely admit, honored governor, that I wanted to get as far as possible from those bad memories. Years passed, during which I saw Allah's hand move in strange ways. I was amazed to discover, my lord, that the world is filled with secrets that human beings, regardless of how evil, good, ignorant, or learned they are, would never imagine. So things went with me until I found myself having entered the great city of Chengdu, capital of the Jin Kingdom in northern China. Never, my lord, never in my life had I seen the equal of that city apart from Bukhara and possibly Samarkand. Allah has graced that land with water and agriculture, He has blessed its women with beauty and grace and its men with knowledge and wisdom. Its markets were filled with every conceivable kind of goods and all at fair prices. Beyond these things, Allah graced the place with safety and security. The city is surrounded by walls so great, only the Great Wall that surrounds the entire Jin Kingdom is greater. These walls, my lord, if you could see them, you would think that they had been built by a nation of giants; no human nor djinn could penetrate them. Because perfection lies with Allah alone, however, and the will of man matters not at all, there are weaknesses to be found. That nation was under the rule of a man named Xuanzong. As much as the people of Chengdu were blessed with wisdom, their emperor had none. As much as the women of the city were beautiful, the emperor's behavior was reprehensible. As I sojourned through the various districts of the city, I found a massive crowd of people surrounding a cage not fit for an animal. A man had been placed in this cage by order of the emperor and was allowed neither food nor water.

"When I enquired, I learned that he was a warrior from a Mongol tribe, and his name was Temujin. He was taken prisoner by the khan of the Niman tribe who was a great enemy of Temujin's house. He hated this man so much that he did not want to grant him a warrior's death as would be customary among the tribes of the steppes. Instead, he wanted this Temujin to live until his body wasted away, to make him an example for any who would dare to attack the Niman. The khan found no greater disgrace than to sell this man as a slave to a Jin merchant. The merchant, in turn, gave him as a gift to Emperor Xuanzong. When his high priest informed him that the appearance of the Mongol warrior was a portent of woe and destruction for the Jin Empire and to all kingdoms of this world, the Emperor had him caged like an animal and put on public display. I keep no secrets from you, my lord. When I saw this poor man's circumstances and his treatment, I felt compassion for him, and I remembered the old saying: have mercy on the humiliated. I held fast to my faith and put my trust in Allah, then before the dawn prayer, I went to the cage which was surrounded by three guards. I offered them a dinar each to allow me to approach the man inside. They all agreed. When I got to the cage, I gave this man a piece of bread and a drink of water under the cover of darkness; none of the three guards noticed. I prayed for him, that Allah would set him free if his imprisonment was unjust. Before Allah, I swear, my lord, a man who has tasted injustice will not allow it to be imposed on another, not even his worst enemy; without doubt, this poor warrior had become my neighbor in misfortune.

"Here is where the unexpected happened. He grabbed my hand, this imprisoned warrior. I thought he intended me some harm, but he simply asked my name. When I told him, as I quivered there, he told me – in a language I understood, it resembled the language of the Turks – 'I will not forget what you have done for me. When I am free of this prison, when I become king over all the kings of this world, I will search for you, and I will pay you back many, many times over.'

"I assure you, my lord, that what I say is true. I nearly laughed at this poor prisoner's words. He was in such bad shape, I doubted he would live more than a day or two. This man promised me rewards once he becomes the king of kings? But I did not laugh; I simply translated Allah's words for him: 'It is for the sake of Allah that we feed you, we need no reward nor any thanks from you.' That is how I left him.

"Some days passed, and I forgot about that imprisoned warrior. Life's concerns occupied my time until I heard that he had managed to escape from prison. Then I learned that his wife, Borte, was the one who helped him... but that is another story.

"I swear before Allah, my lord, that I was overjoyed when I heard he was free. I prayed that Allah would guide him to a righteous path. You may imagine, my lord, my shock when, several years later, several horse-mounted warriors came to me in Kashgar after it was conquered by the Mongols to tell me that they had been searching the world over for me for years at the order of their Great Khan. Of course, I did not understand things then. Even the warriors who came for me did not know the reason why their khan had sent them to search for me. Mongol warriors are known for their blind, unquestioning obedience to their commanders' orders. I went with them; I had no other choice. They eventually brought me to the camp of their king, a man called Genghis Khan. My shock at what I saw has no bounds, my lord. When I met the king, he was that same poor prisoner I had helped long years before in the city of Chengdu. He had searched for me as promised so he could reward me."

Silence filled the governor's chambers once Mohamed bin Ishaq Elbukhari completed his fantastic tale of how a Muslim man from Bukhara, after decades of itinerant travel, became part of the Mongol king's inner circle. It was only a moment before the governor broke the silence to enquire about something else that had been bothering him, something he had seen in the market.

"I've heard that Otrar has never seen a caravan like yours before, and that you brought the highest quality goods with you."

"Yes, my lord, and please accept my gratitude as well as that of the entire caravan for your generosity in granting us room to set up and for opening the gates in your great city walls to us. I have brought with me some gifts that I pray to Allah will bring you some pleasure. With your permission, my lord, I will have them brought in."

Yanal Khan gestured to his doorman who immediately opened the doors to the council chamber, permitting dozens of servants bearing chests filled with the finest spices, perfumes, and cloth of silk and wool in a display so grand, the governor nearly leapt from his seat so his hands could examine what his eyes feasted upon.

"There is one other thing, with your permission, my lord." Mohamed added haltingly.

"Bring all you have." Yanal Khan told him, his eyes darting between his interlocutor and the chests overflowing with rich gifts.

"My lord, before Allah I tell you I am embarrassed by what I must ask, but it is not for me. Another man, a stranger who joined our caravan a few days ago as we approached the city, made this request of me. If I had not – along with Princess Yasimi – found him to be very knowledgeable and of good moral constitution, I would not have accepted the burden of this message I now bear."

"What could be in this message?"

Even more hesitantly, Mohamed answered the governor's question. "Your pardon, my lord, but the source of the message took an oath from me that I would not reveal its contents except in the presence of Emir Jalal-Eddin."

"Come now, man! Who could this companion be, able to set conditions on my council chamber?" The governor, now furious, cried out.

"I beg your pardon, my lord…"

"Regardless, Emir Jalal-Eddin is busy at the present time. For me to call him here to hear a message from an unknown man is unreasonable, no matter how well educated or righteous you claim he may be!"

"Glory be to Allah who sows his secrets within whom he wills among his servants!" the merchant sheikh replied, shocked by the governor's response. He continued, "Abdel-Rahman told me this would be your response to his request, then he told me that I should wait a little, and Emir Jalal-Eddin will come of his own accord."

No sooner had this statement left bin Ishaq's mouth than the chamber door opened and Emir Jalal-Eddin Manguberdi entered, accompanied by his nephew Mahmoud bin Mamdoud. They had come to inform Yanal Khan that they would be leaving Otrar that day for their sojourn outside the Khwarezmian Empire. The governor could not hide his surprise at what had just happened. "Is this some sort of plot, or was it arranged by demons and djinn?" He was both suspicious and apprehensive, and the Emir noticed the change in his demeanor. The greater surprise was felt by all when Mohamed bin Ishaq Elbukhari delivered Abdel-Rahman's message.

"Impossible!" cried the governor.

His vizier Khalid bin Mansour added, "How could this unknown man have succeeded where all the nation's scholars have come up short?"

Everyone disparaged what the merchant sheikh told them. Everyone other than the Emir and his nephew who sought a way out, one that would save them as well as Nouran Khatoun from their trip to Mongol territory. They were perfectly willing to hear what the stranger had to tell them, for he claimed to have a lawful way out of the oath Sultan Alaa-Eddin Mohamed made to his wife: that she would spend three nights outside his lands. The path he offered would save the Sultan from forswearing himself and save the his wife from spending three nights outside the Khwarezmian Empire.

(22)
A Few Days Earlier

Following the death of the Mongol commander, Murad kept to himself, observing everything. After what he had seen but could not comprehend, he found he had nothing to say. It was as if the situation in which he found himself after being thrown from the tower was not enough on its own. He also had to watch, with his own eyes, as that dark, amorphous creature killed a man with the mere touch of its ethereal hand. There was nothing he could do other than watch and hope that this was nothing more than a nightmare and he would wake any moment to find himself still in Riyadh, in his own comfortable bed in his cool, air-conditioned room. But reality would not bend to his desires. Things certainly seemed dreamlike, but something inside whispered to him that he would continue to watch... and watch... and watch. It didn't take long for Murad to realize that as strange as this was, it wasn't a dream. He could tell it was a new reality, one both unfamiliar and incomprehensible. If he wanted to save himself from the clutches of this puzzle, he would have to *see*.

"You look, but you don't *see*." What was he looking at that he did not see? Murad started spending time brooding over this question once Abdel-Rahman made it clear that – although he was the only person who could see, hear, and speak with Murad – for some reason, he did not want to help. Or so it seemed. Rather than help, Abdel-Rahman piled conundrums on top of the mysteries he already faced.

The caravan got back underway shortly after burying the body of the Mongol warrior, and Murad started to take more notice of the things happening around him. No one talked about what happened, for one thing. They all accepted the simple idea offered at first, that it was simply his time. What surprised Murad was that Abdel-Rahman, who had seen the same thing he had and knew the truth, did not try to explain things to anyone; neither to the Mongol princess nor the caravan's sheikh, who had stepped forward to take charge of the situation. After spending some time considering the situation carefully, Murad realized that silence was probably Abdel-Rahman's best course of action. After all, what could he say? An invisible creature killed the caravan commander? Who would believe him? No, silence was his only real option. *I wonder if this is why Abdel-Rahman says so little. Does he see more than everyone else, things that are hard for him to internalize? Is this the secret behind his silence?*

***

Two more days of travel brought the caravan to Otrar. Two days is not long, however two significant events occurred that drew Murad's attention, making the matter of Abdel-Rahman even more perplexing.

The first happened the day after Tenukei was killed. Murad had noticed the odd diversity of the Mongol caravan. Most, if not all, of the merchants were Muslims while the fighters were more of a mixed group. A few were easily identified as Christians because they wore crosses around their necks. Some of the others were Buddhists; he had seen them praying to a small statue of the Buddha. Most of the warriors, though, followed a faith Murad had never heard of, but as he listened to them talk, he was able to determine that it was a faith followed by most Mongols, including Genghis Khan, founded on the belief in a single god named Tengri, who they called the "Lord of the Blue Sky." What struck Murad as most strange, was that, despite this apparent variety of beliefs, the people were not polarized by religion. Most of the warriors and merchants worked together in harmony; the warrior who took command of the guards after Tenukei was killed was one of the few Christians, and the majority – followers of the Mongol faith – did not complain. In the same way, the new Christian commander himself never had a problem taking orders from the Muslim sheikh who led the merchants. The amazing thing about this was that when the harmony and accord among the party collapsed, it was a dispute among the Muslim merchants. One of them, a man called Akrama, turned some of the merchants against Mohamed bin Ishaq, trying to have him removed as their Sheikh. His reasoning was that bin

Ishaq was committing heresy, bid'ah, by basing the sharia decisions he made for the Muslim merchants on reasoning and analogy – ra'i and qiyas – rather than relying solely on the text of the Qur'an and the record of the Prophet's words and deeds. His efforts succeeded in dividing the caravan's Muslim merchants into two camps; one following Akrama in contesting the use of qiyas when making decisions, the other standing with Mohamed bin Ishaq – bringing the caravan to a halt until a final decision could be reached.

None of the warriors tried to interfere; their job was to guard the caravan. The merchants' affairs were their own. No one else had the right to get involved unless the merchants accepted their arbitration. This is how Genghis Khan ran things, and so the dispute between Akrama's faction and Ishaq's faction continued – until the second event occurred, ending the conflict and bringing back the caravan's general harmony. Akrama allowed Abdel-Rahman to ask him a question:

"Your objection to Sheikh Mohamed bin Ishaq Elbukhari is that he uses reasoning and analogy, and you claim that this is not permitted." Abdel-Rahman said, opening the dialog.

"Yes. This is correct. There is no reasoning or analogy in sharia law! Adherence to the text is the only way!" Akrama answered, and several of his faction chimed in with their support:

"How can we accept a heretic like Mohamed bin Ishaq as our sheikh, our elder, when he leads us astray in his dealings with us?" and "No, Allah as our witness, this must not be!"

The merchants continued to cry out in this vein until Abdel-Rahman asked the question that caught Akrama and his companions off-guard in its simplicity: "How would you rule in the case of someone who accuses an innocent man without bringing forth four witnesses?"

"What are you talking about, man? What does this have to do with the topic at hand?" Akrama demanded, resentful of both the question and the questioner.

"Answer me, and I will tell you."

"The ruling would be as Allah's book provides: he would be given eighty lashes and his testimony would no longer be valid."

"And what evidence supports what you say?" the sheikh asked.

Akrama's only response was to stare at Abdel-Rahman, surprised by the question that had seemed so guileless. His companions, too, grumbled among themselves about this perceived pointless waste of their time. Even Mohamed bin Ishaq was a little embarrassed by this question; so simple that it should only be asked of someone with little understanding of fiqh, Islamic jurisprudence.

"Listen, man. If you are ignorant of Allah's book, I advise you to learn something of it before asking others so you might have something to contribute." Akrama turned his back on Abdel-Rahman and addressed himself to Mohamed bin Ishaq: "I do not count this against you, Abu Elhassan. We made you our Qadi, it is up to us to remove you. It would be best for you to save face by voluntarily stepping down. If you don't…"

"You did not answer the question." Abdel-Rahman said, cutting Akrama off and drawing his ire.

"What's wrong with you? Are you crazy, man?" he shouted, "Leave us! If you do not, I swear by Allah almighty that I will remove you from this caravan!"

"Who would eject someone from this caravan without my permission?" Yasimi said, approaching the gathering of merchants when she heard the shouting.

"Your pardon, your highness, but this is an issue between the merchants only; your grandfather, Genghis Khan gave orders that these matters should be left to…"

"There is no need at this time to remind me of Genghis Khan's orders." The princess interjected. "But this does not give you the right to mistreat my guests."

"Your pardon, your highness, such was not my intent."

"He has asked you a simple question, why do you not answer him?"

Akrama looked to Abdel-Rahman who stood as he had been, waiting for an answer to his question.

"Evidence for this ruling comes from Sura Al-Noor: 'For those who accuse chaste women and do not provide four witnesses: give them eighty lashes and accept not their testimony henceforth for they are defiantly disobedient.' Now, your highness, I have answered your guest's question. Will you now order him to leave us and our affairs alone so we can have an end to this matter?"

"But you have not yet provided evidence." Abdel-Rahman answered in a quiet voice. Before he even finished his sentence, Akrama and his companions all began speaking at once, fed up with this ignorant man trying to deny common knowledge.

"Are you deaf, man, or do you deny Allah's book?"

"The verse you recited from Sura Al-Noor speaks about falsely accusing chaste women. My question was about a man. Where is the verse that speaks about how to punish someone who has made false accusations against a chaste man without witnesses? It seems that you have used qiyas – a practice you claim is forbidden when by Mohamed bin Ishaq does it – without thinking about it when you answered me. You have placed the male in where a female is mentioned – chaste men instead of chaste women as indicated in the verse. If qiyas is forbidden, as you claim, then the text must be taken literally, and one must not treat someone who falsely accuses a chaste man as one would the accuser of a chaste woman."

As Abdel-Rahman finished speaking, the companions of Mohamed bin Ishaq seemed to swell up before Akrama, who was stammering, unable to respond to the stranger whom he had been taunting and calling ignorant a moment before. Even his companions, who had supported him from the outset, were quick to desert him one after another. Soon there were none left demanding Mohamed bin Ishaq Elbukhari be removed from the position of elder sheikh among the merchants of the caravan. From that moment on, no one heard a sound from Akrama, and no one paid him any heed.

***

The second event that drew Murad's attention happened the next day, just before sunset prayer, when he saw Abdel-Rahman looking south, gazing at the distant horizon. The sky was periodically lit by flashes of lightening, and the thunder that followed was so faint it was almost impossible to hear from the caravan. For a little while, Abdel-Rahman stood still, seeming deep in thought, then he suddenly spun to face Mohamed bin Ishaq and Princess Yasimi and told them that a severe lightning storm was headed their way and that they could not outrun it. He advised them to make preparations. At first, the Sheikh was unconvinced. Even if the prediction was correct, this would not be the first storm to strike the caravan; most storms didn't even require the caravan to stop traveling. Abdel-Rahman insisted, however, and warned that the consequences of ignoring him would be dire. Bin Ishaq consulted the commander of the guard, who disagreed with Abdel-Rahman, instead ordering the caravan to continue, disregarding the warnings of the stranger who had only been with the caravan for a few days. They had no idea how knowledgeable he was concerning the weather. But Yasimi, whose confidence in this man had been growing steadily since he joined them, demanded that they listen to his advice – though this drew the ire of the sheikh and the commander both.

"My lady, I have assumed responsibility for this caravan since Tenukei died. I will be accountable for its safety before the king of kings, Genghis Khan."

The warrior tried to explain to her that stopping now and following this stranger's instructions would be insane – he wanted them to gather up all jewelry and swords and lay them out on the ground around the caravan and stack the spears on top the piles. Then he wanted them to disperse their livestock and the rest of the animals some distance away from the caravan itself. Yasimi, however, stood her ground. She placed her full trust in Abdel-Rahman and his warning. She got what she wanted, despite the leaders of the guard and the merchants. Just as night fell, a storm unlike anything they had encountered on their journey broke overhead. Chaos broke out as lightning crashed into the ground around the caravan, and thunder roared, filling their hearts with terror.

When the storm crashed into them, Yasimi sought shelter under a nearby tree as some of the others had done. Abdel-Rahman grabbed her and bodily forced her to lay flat on the ground just before the lightning struck the tree and set it on fire, electrocuting everyone who had stayed under it. He directed everyone to lie down where they were, pressed to the ground, just as he was. Some followed his advice, others did not. The lightning flashed from the sky to strike the spears that were erected, as Abdel-Rahman had ordered, over the mounds of jewelry and swords, stacked on piles of stone and wood and dispersed at regular intervals. No one knew why he gave this order at the time, but they quickly saw the wisdom. When the storm hit, they could see for themselves how these spears protected them from the lightning strikes; each bolt hit the erected spears and left the prone humans alone.

And so it went until the storm finally abated. They lost a few camels – and a few merchants and guards who hadn't listened to Abdel-Rahman's advice. But the storm wasn't the last tragedy of the night. With the end of the storm, one of the surviving warriors went to retrieve the sword he had cast into one of the piles of weapons and jewelry; the instant he touched it, he was electrocuted – stretched out flat on his back, instantly dead in full view of his companions who all froze, terrified by what they had just seen.

What came next was harder for the survivors to bear than the storm itself had been. What they beheld could only have been the work of a great sorcerer or a great gift from the elder gods. Some of the Muslim merchants even began to whisper amongst themselves that the stranger who joined them might be Khidr, the ancient prophet, particularly since he wore a green turban, and green was the prophet's color. It wasn't long before this became the prevailing theory among everyone in the caravan; they had all seen Abdel-Rahman rushing to the young guard who was struck dead in front of everyone. The green-turbaned man started pressing on the guard's chest and blowing in his mouth – which everyone thought was crazy at first, but then they were all awestruck when the guard returned to life. They couldn't believe what they had just witnessed.

"Abdel-Rahman brought the Mongol guard back to life after he died!"

***

These two events established Abdel-Rahman's place in the caravan in everyone's eyes, including Mohamed bin Ishaq Elbukhari and Yasimi. The two of them had been conversing with him from the beginning, hoping to learn everything they could from this man's seemingly bottomless well of wisdom. Several of the merchants went so far as to offer him gifts out of their goods to show their gratitude. He strenuously refused all. When they asked him to pray that their business be blessed, he would tell them that Allah requires no intercessor between Himself and His followers, reminding them of the verse: If my servants ask thee about me, I am close by and I answer the prayers of those who call upon me.

The whole thing seemed extremely strange to Murad Qutuz. Not because what Abdel-Rahman did was odd, but because to him, there was clear reasoning behind everything and none of it had to do with magic or supernatural powers. In Murad's view, what Abdel-Rahman had done was nothing more than practical application of science. Any child who was a decent student could have done the same thing. Abdel-Rahman's knowledge of the approaching storm came from counting the seconds between the visible lightening and the crash of thunder, knowing sound traveled at one mile for every five seconds. By repeating this exercise several times and comparing the distance, he could tell if the storm was approaching.

Ordering everyone to pile the swords and jewelry in mounds with the spears standing above them was a way of dealing with the electrical nature of lightning – he made grounding rods of the spears which drew the lightning strikes. And reviving the Mongol guard, that was just CPR. No magic, no act of the gods, no miracles. Anyone who knew science could do the same thing, there was nothing strange or magical to it at all.

"It is just about having knowledge of the reasons behind what happened. That's why some observers saw magic or paranormal powers and you saw science. They saw what they saw based on their level of understanding; at yours, you saw something different. They saw the facts as they understood them, you saw the facts as they are." Abdel-Rahman's voice told him in his mind, demonstrating that he could communicate with Murad telepathically. There was no need for him to use his mouth, just as Murad, currently incorporeal, had no physical mouth with which to speak.

There were other things Murad Qutuz was starting to figure out, things that were incomprehensible when he first appeared in this place, but were becoming as obvious as the lightning had been.

"You're like me!" he said to Abdel-Rahman, "You aren't from this time! How could I have missed that before now? How did I fail to notice that you didn't react when I asked about an airport in Otrar? You seemed to know what "airport" meant already. Just now, you calculated the speed of sound from the thunder, you used CPR to save that guard; these things come from science that hasn't been discovered yet! You have knowledge from a different time. But how? The only explanation would be that you are like me, you come from the future. But you can manifest physically and interact with the people here! How?"

Abdel-Rahman smiled, pleased by Murad's deductions. "You looked, and you saw. You heard, and you listened – even to things I did not say. You connected things, you observed… now you started down the path to your goal."

***

Following these two events, the caravan approached Otrar's city walls. Abdel-Rahman had earned enough favor to ask Mohamed bin Ishaq to deliver a message to the governor, Yanal Khan and Emir Jalal-Eddin Manguberdi. More than that, he gave Murad hope in his suffering, and Princes Yasimi was able to learn from a man like none she had met before.

"Why do people call Otrar 'the City of the Second Teacher?"

"Abu Nasser Mohamed bin Mohamed bin Usalgh bin Tarkhan was born and raised there. People call him Al-Farabi or Alpharabius; Farab is the ancient name for Otrar. He is also known as the Second Teacher because of his mastery of philosophy; Aristotle is the First Teacher." Abdel-Rahman told Yasimi when she asked.

"I remember Rustum bin Yazdashir told me a little about him and his ideas about the virtuous city, but I didn't understand any of it."

"All you need to know is what Al-Farabi meant by the term 'the virtuous city'. To him, such a city would be filled with people who seek joy through their love of wisdom and coexistence rather than through conflict and discord. He juxtaposed this vision first against a city of ignorance whose people indulge themselves in the quest for riches and pleasures. He also compared it to a misguided city, where the people have the same knowledge as those in the virtuous city, but they follow the path of the ignorant city. To Al-Farabi, this last was the worst; an ignorant person can be given knowledge, which solves the problem. The misguided people in the other city are lost; they know what is right, but they choose to be willfully ignorant."

Yasimi continued to ask questions and Abdel-Rahman continued to explain things to her until they set up camp near the walls of Otrar, when he went into the city with the merchants.

(23)
A Simple Solution

News of the man who accompanied the Mongol caravan spread throughout the city's residents. People said that he had an Islamic solution to Emira Nouran's troubles that would save her from being forced to leave the Khwarezmian Empire's territory without forcing the Sultan to foreswear his oath. Everyone wanted to know more; how could a stranger no one had ever heard of, who came from beyond the Abode of Islam in the company of a caravan sent by barbarian tribes, succeed where the most esteemed and privileged scholars of Bukhara and Samarkand had failed? Could anyone have anything more to say once the High Qadi of the Khwarezmian Empire, Abu Abdel-Aziz Yahya bin Rihan had made his ruling and had his say? In truth, many of the people did not believe that this man, this Abdel-Rahman dhu Elemama Elkhadra "of the green turban" (or so they named him, lacking a way to attach him to a person or place), could have discovered something new. Most people thought only the elite would even want to make the attempt, hoping to gain some honor even if they failed. Despite the prevailing belief, curiosity filled them; and some harbored a deep desire for Abdel-Rahman dhu Elemama Elkhadra to succeed, if for no other reason than to spite the High Qadi who, along with his subordinate qadis, burdened the people with rulings throughout the Khwarezmian Empire.

The time had come, the moment the people, particularly those in and around the Governor's Palace, had been waiting for: Abdel-Rhaman strode through the wooden doors on his way to the governor's audience chamber where Emir Jalal-Eddin, Vizier Khalid bin Mansour, and Otrar's Qadi, Jaber bin Khayzran, Nouran Khatoun's grandson, Emir Mahmoud bin Mamdoud waited, praying Abdel-Rahman's claims were true and he would bring them a solution to his grandmother's situation.

***

Yanal Khan inspected the man who entered his chamber; the man's appearance did not inspire confidence. He had a penetrating gaze and a straight back; he made no pretense of bowing to the Governor or Emir Jalal-Eddin when he came in, as was customary. His appearance and demeanor combined to make the governor feel like this stranger from outside Muslim lands was hiding something.

"What is your name, man?" Jalal-Eddin began.

"Abdel-Rahman."

"Abdel-Rahman son of whom?"

"Abdel-Rahman son of Abdel-Rahman."

"You claim to have an opinion that diverges from the one agreed upon by the scholars of Khwarezm concerning his Majesty the Sultan's oath. Before we hear what you have to say, why don't you tell us under whom you have studied?"

"I have learned from every creature in creation." Abdel-Rahman replied pointedly.

As the questioning began, Emir Jalal-Eddin and his companions started to feel like they were in the presence of an ignorant plaintiff who had come only to waste their valuable time; a man of no family who just wanted to be the center of attention.

"Fine. Go on, man. Tell us what you have – if you have anything new to offer on the matter." Yanal Khan jumped in, out of patience and just wanting to get this pointless meeting over with.

Abdel-Rahman paid no heed to the governor. He just looked at the Emir who nodded to him, signaling him to have his say.

"The Sultan made an oath: his wife would spend three nights outside the empire. This she must do if he does not wish to foreswear his oath…"

The babble of voices filled the room at this pronouncement, people grumbling at what he had said – including Mohamed bin Ishaq who was profoundly embarrassed for having testified to Abdel-Rahman's scholarship and showing complete confidence in him, but now…

"Really! This is what you bring before us?" Shouted Yanal Khan over the noise. He addressed the Emir who was covering his disappointment with rage. "I knew this man came just to taunt us!"

"However," Abdel-Rahman continued, unruffled by the clamor around him. "This does not mean that the Sultan's wife must leave Khwarezm. She does not even need to leave the city of Bukhara."

"What are you trying to do here, man? Did you not just say..."

"Your pardon, governor. Why don't we let him finish before we decide he means ill?" Emir Jalal-Eddin interrupted, then went on, addressing Abdel-Rahman. "Please explain what you mean, if you have a point beyond what we have understood."

"*Mosques belong to Allah, invoke not anyone alongside Allah.*" Abdel-Rahman recited. "The solution to this dilemma rests within this verse from the Holy Qur'an."

Jalal-Eddin immediately turned to Qadi Jaber to see if he understood Abdel-Rahman's intent, but the Qadi was just as lost and simply raised his eyebrows.

"Mosques belong to Allah and no one else. They are not among the Sultan's possessions. On that basis, Nouran Khatoun can stay in any mosque for three days, and thus meet the requirements of the Sultan's oath."

With this pronouncement, Mohamed bin Ishaq shouted his praise to Allah and heaved a deep sigh, relieved that he had not lost face in public, and in particular, in the eyes of the governor who was now looking to the Qadi of Otrar who, in turn, was standing in silent shock at what he had just heard. The man had

148

indeed discovered something where he and all the scholars of the Khwarezmian Empire had failed. His solution was perfect in its simplicity and cleverness; the Qadi had no choice but to concur with the ruling offered by Abdel-Rahman, though it was an embarrassment to him and Qadi Abu Abdel-Rahman Yahya bin Rihan, and more importantly – it would enrage Turkan Khatoun!

(24)

As Time Goes By

The present... the past... the future... what meaning do these words hold? Murad couldn't tell the difference between them anymore – or at least, he couldn't come up with a useful definition for the terms. The present simply means what is happening now, with him in this strange, inexplicable form. The present is, simultaneously, the past, in relation to the life he had been living up until recently. What about his personal past? How should he see that now? Is it a future that hasn't yet occurred, or is it still the past because it has happened to him and now it is done and over with? These simple concepts of time no longer held any meaning for him. As for the future... what could that even mean? The whole thing had become an impossible conundrum with no apparent solution. However, in the days that had passed since he came to in Central Asia, the tentacles of despair that had gripped his miserable existence had begun to loosen, releasing him from their embrace, especially since he found hope... since he discovered that he was not the only one not of this time!

***

Murad didn't try to speak to Abdel-Rahman again. He was content to simply observe everything happening around him, trying to puzzle out the story behind these events. He hoped to find something else that would help him understand the truth behind what was happening to him and around him. Obviously, he was seeing a period of history he had read little about, though he had heard often, as many do, about the Mongol attack on Muslim territory and how the Mongols destroyed cities and slaughtered the innocent. What he saw today was, or at least seemed to be, before those terrifying events took place. Here he was in a Mongol caravan, half Muslim, coming for peaceful trade. *When will everything shift and the tragedies begin?* he started to wonder, *I wish I could warn the poor people about what those Mongols will do to them. But I'm just an observer, there's nothing I can do. I am just as powerless as someone sitting at home watching a Ramadan miniseries on television, unable to alter what the show's writers created and the director's cameras filmed.*

Things were calm around Murad. Once the Mongol caravan stopped in Otrar, some of the merchants wanted to stay so they could sell the rest of their goods, while others preferred to move on to Bukhara with Princess Yasimi and Mohamed bin Ishaq. Emir Jalal-Eddin had offered to accompany them there with his mother, Nouran Khatoun, and his nephew, Mahmoud. His generous invitation came after he learned that the Mongol ruler's granddaughter was being escorted by the caravan and that the Mongol merchant sheikh carried a letter for his father, Sultan Alaa-Eddin. Jalal-Eddin was overjoyed by the safe and religiously acceptable solution that Abdel-Rahman had discovered. Not only did he provide his mother with a way out of her conundrum, he saved Jalal-Eddin from the problems that would have come from traveling outside his father's empire and staying three long nights in unknown territory surrounded by strangers who were subject to Mongol rule. Thus the trip to Bukhara went smoothly with no great friction between the Mongols and Jalal-Eddin's party. Mohamed bin Ishaq acted as the point of contact between the two groups, and Yasimi was overcome with curiosity that pushed her to go to the Khwarezmian caravan uninvited to learn about them and their customs and to spend a little time among their warriors; she even joined in their horse games from time to time, when the caravan was halted for the evening or for a rest. None of the Khwarezmians were accustomed to a girl acting this way, particularly a princess; her behavior was a novelty to some and earned censure from others. Yasimi didn't care much about what they thought, regardless of bin Ishaq's frequent admonitions. She liked showing off her brilliant horsemanship. Even Jalal-Eddin praised her skill once, when he saw her best many of his warriors in a game of buzkashi. In the game, the object is to carry a slaughtered goat on horseback to a specific point, run a circle around the spot and then run back to throw the goat into a hole on the opposite side of the field. The most amazing part of this was that Yasimi had never played the game; she had never even seen it played, when she asked if she could join in. Their acceptance came with great astonishment, but it came quickly, if only for the novelty of the thing: a Mongol princess who came from the land of barbarians, who wanted to compete with the men at their own game. Jalal-Eddin tried to talk her out of playing, afraid she would get hurt because of the games' rough nature. In the end, seeing her determination to participate, he gave in to her request – especially since Mohamed bin Ishaq offered no objection and seemed indifferent to something that could cause her harm.

The game started by placing the slaughtered goat in the middle of the field. The riders dashed forward to snatch the goat from the ground, but they were slower off the start than usual, following Jalal-Eddin's orders to take it a little easy on the young lady and allow her to get the goat and make a few points. Surely, they thought, she would not last more than a round or two. Once the game started, though, Yasimi did not press her horse forward to the goat, instead she contented herself with following behind the other horsemen, giving the appearance that she was scared. One of the men, the first to grab the goat from the ground, took pity on the young princess and tried to give it to her after reassuring her that no harm would come to her, but she refused.

The game went on for several rounds like this until the horsemen began to forget about the Mongol girl. She was just watching, not doing anything, so they eventually went back to their normal play style, getting rougher with one another and ignoring the girl. When the seventh round came, the signal to begin was given, Yasimi surged forward on her horse, shocking everyone. She left all the guards in the dust as she sped by, the men agape in disbelief. Yasimi made no move to slow as the men had been doing when they approached the goat. She charged ahead at speed and, leaning her upper body precariously towards the ground, grabbed the goat as she passed, then sat back up straight, leaving everyone slack-jawed; they couldn't believe the girl's dexterity. None of the Khwarezmian men could do it so quickly. With her speed and dexterity, she racked up point after point until the game ended and she came in first place. That young lady had defeated the most skilled warriors of Khwarezm, the best of the buzkashi players. Her skill was equal to any horseman guarding her caravan; she had demonstrated to all the players that she could anticipate their actions. Without a doubt, Yasimi had their attention now. She did what she had to do, after observing their style of play, to clear the way and be sure no one could take the goat from her. Even Emir Jalal-Eddin and his nephew Mahmoud who was unaccustomed to watching buzkashi could see it. For Mahmoud, the sight of the beautiful Mongol princess, at most a year or two older than he was, playing with his uncle's warriors – and winning! – was incredible. She had his attention and his admiration.

"How did she gain such incredible skill on horseback?" Mahmoud asked Mohamed bin Ishaq, the latter beaming with pride and joy as though the girl in the game was his own daughter. The answer was a surprise to Mahmoud: all Mongol children learn to ride horses before they learn to walk. With this upbringing, by the time they grow up, the horse becomes an extension of their bodies.

"It is this that makes Mongol horsemen and horsewomen the best in the world on horseback. Indeed, there are none capable of matching a mounted Mongol."

Mahmoud bin Mamdoud was enthralled by this, but Emir Jalal-Eddin felt a rising concern. If a Mongol girl of no more than fourteen summers could do this, what could an adult Mongol horseman, practiced in the art of war, do? The son of the Khwarezmian Sultan hoped that the day would never come when he was forced to find out.

***

Through the entire journey to Bukhari, Abdel-Rahman walked alone some distance away from both caravans and out of sight. He rarely spoke with members of either group, though Emir Jalal-Eddin and his mother Nouran persisted in inviting him to eat with them every time the caravan stopped. He also avoided pressure from both Yasimi and Mohamed bin Ishaq to accompany them in the caravan so they could enjoy his company and conversation and learn from the expansive experience and knowledge that he had demonstrated to them on more than one occasion. Even Murad Qutuz was unable to talk to him beyond one conversation a few days after the caravan left Otrar. When Yasimi took on the Khwarezmian guards – and won – Murad felt like his sympathies lay with the girl as he watched, she was so brave and determined. For a moment, he wished she could see him and talk to him as she could with Abdel-Rahman.

"It is no great secret that she is favored among Genghis Khan's granddaughters, even if her parentage was somewhat dubious." Abdel-Rahman told Murad, suddenly appearing at his side.

"He loves her? Yet he abandons her to go, at such a tender age, on a journey from which she might not return?

"She is not all that young by the standards of this time. Her grandmother, Borte, was even younger when she married her grandfather. Genghis Khan sent her this far away because he loves her, because he understands that, regardless of her beauty, intelligence, and courage, she will always be a child of dubious parentage – and that she has incurred the curse of Tabtinkar."

"Dubious...? And who or what is Tabtinkar?"

Murad didn't understand what Abdel-Rahman was talking about. He waited for an answer to his question, but his odd companion made no attempt to clarify things. Instead, he changed the subject to something Murad saw as completely unrelated.

"One of the strangest things I've heard people – many people – say is: 'History says...' As if history speaks for itself instead it being recorded by human beings."

"Huh?"

"Each person sees events from their own unique outlook. Each person sees things that others do not – and this begs the question: where does the truth lay? You, for example, what are the facts concerning what happened to you? What are the facts concerning the things that have been happening around you?"

Murad replied with his own question, "Why do I get the feeling that you know more than you are letting on? You already know the answer to many of these questions, yet you do nothing to ease my mind!"

"Throughout the ages, many nations have rewritten their histories." Abdel-Rahman continued. "because they fear the facts hidden within those histories. Often, lies are the only way to ease a mind or conscience, but they remain lies. One who seeks the facts must be ready to bear the pain they bring. The only path is to love the truth more than oneself."

There was no way Murad could tell what question Abdel-Rahman was answering; it felt like he had gone back to speaking in riddles. What truth and what pain was he talking about? Did any pain exist greater than what he was going through now? Is there any pain greater than confusion and incomprehension? No matter how painful the world could be, nothing was worse than ignorance! For a moment, Murad felt the urge to ask him defiantly: *Tell me, what must I do to understand the facts of what happened to me?* but he didn't. Something inside him feared the answer.

(25)
Possibility and Ability

After placing the herbs on the brass tray, heated by the stones beneath, he sat before the dense smoke as it began to fill the tent. This was the method, passed down to him through his ancestors, he used to enter the other world. It was a secret that must never be revealed, one known only to a tiny fraction of humanity, and it was the key to his power. In that world, Tabtinkar was not bound by his body, so he could travel with the spirits. He could cross the barriers of time; the walls between past and present, between present and future had no meaning. Most of the time, he could see with complete clarity; but at times the image was blurred, and he had to puzzle out the meaning of what he saw. In either case, he saw what no one else could and he knew what others would not know until it had come to pass. In this lay the secret of his power and his unmatched strength. As the years passed, as the number of times he visited that strange world grew, and as he refined the spirit herbs he used – adding compounds he learned of in his years of travel and the knowledge gleaned through decades of experimentation – he was able to communicate with beings no one before him had ever managed to. He called them the shadow people.

"You should not have killed Tenukei!" the shaman said, condemning the action.

"You should not have given an order I did not approve of." The disembodied shadow responded.

"Is that why you had to kill one of the warriors of the King of all Kings of this Earth, Genghis Khan?"

"I wanted to send you a message you would not forget. You must always remember who it is you are working with. I have told you before, my dear shaman, that our battle is not one of Earth-bound warriors. We have left this battle to Temujin and his followers. *Our* fight is only understood be the very few.

"If Tenukei had not died at my hands, Abdel-Rahman would have been able to kill him before your horseman could take him down. My dear friend, do you not know that when intellect and brute force clash, intellect always wins. If this were not a universal constant, humanity would have gone extinct long ago." The being changed the subject, "Now, my shaman, there is a new factor in this equation, one that should not exist."

"Didn't you tell me before that you would take care of him? Did you not? Perhaps you could not."

"I am observing, shaman. Observing."

As the amorphous shape uttered the final word, the scene before Tabtinkar shifted, showing him a different world. It was a future full of magic and miracles: people flying in metal birds, able to watch events on the other side of the planet through mirrors. Tabtinkar saw a man with indistinct features living in an Arab land. This wasn't the first time he had seen a strange scene like this, but this time there were some differences. The world was not the same as it had been. Many things had not come to pass, others that should have did not, but the people still went about life as usual, all except this strange man – he seemed confused. He looked around himself constantly and asked questions about the world he saw that was not as it should be. Perplexed, he kept looking for something that no longer existed, something he had lost.

"Things were not as they had been." Tabtinkar said, commenting on what he had seen this time.

"Yes, shaman. Everything can be changed."

"Is this what you were observing?"

"No, not this. I was watching what did not change."

The old shaman didn't understand. *What did not change?* Don't people always pay attention to change? When did the unchanging become the object of observation?

"Nothing shall be that was not. Nothing shall pass but that which has already passed. The secret of this universe is not in the things that change. The true secret is hidden in the fixed points. When the secret is revealed to you, shaman, you will be granted possibility, and with possibility, comes ability. Only then will we be able to take out Abdel-Rahman and the stranger. Only then we shall have victory!"

(26)
The Sultan's Mother

News of the green-turbaned Abdel-Rahman spread throughout the city of Bukhara, about him and his fatwa, his Islamic ruling, that saved face for Sultan Alaa-Eddin Mohamed and saved his wife Nouran Khatoun from staying outside the Khwarezmian Empire's territory where she would be in danger of attack from the roaming barbarian tribes. Word spread that the caravan traveling with Emir Jalal-Eddin and his mother was about to arrive, and that Abdel-Rahman would be with them. People from all walks of life desperately curious, wanting to catch a glimpse of the man who had solved a problem that had stumped the greatest Qadi and scholar of the Empire, Abu Abdel-Aziz Yahya bin Rihan. Many others were simply pleased that Nouran Khatoun had returned safe and sound, if for no other reason than to spite the Sultan's mother, Turkan Khatoun, despised because of her extreme generosity towards her tribe, the Kankali. She handed the Kankali the best of the Khwarezmian empire at the expense of the general population, and she preferred her tribesmen for government posts, in trade, in land grants and forfeitures; all the while she increased her tribes power and influence. The tribe's status within the empire had grown under her hand. The Kankali had unlimited influence over merchants, workers, governors, ministers, and judges; even over the Sultan himself. Things had gotten to the point where the people had a saying: if you need something, it is better to know a little boy from the tribe of the Sultan's mother than to know the Sultan himself.

***

Turkan was not happy with the news when it arrived from her brother, the governor of Otrar. Her rage was such that she nearly hurled the golden wine goblet beside her couch at the warrior who brought the terrible message. She had set it there to sip from before Yanal Khan's messenger arrived.

"Oh! You bearer of ill news!" Turkan screamed.

"My lady…"

"Get out of my sight this instant, or I shall have your ugly head removed!"

The warrior withdrew quickly, relieved for a moment by this reprieve.

"Bring me the High Qadi! Bring him now, even if he is in bed having sex!"

Turkan was so agitated that she couldn't sit still. Instead, she paced back and forth across her spacious chambers until bin Rihan came.

"My lady."

"What kind of garbage is this, High Qadi? How could a nobody like this be permitted to issue a fatwa in

Khwarezm, with as many scholars as Khwarezm has? Or has scholarship fled the land?"

"My lady, I heard what happened in Otrar. Truly, I do not know how..."

"Did you not tell me Nouran had no choice but to stay outside the empire? How did this happen?! Where did this man come up with his fatwa?"

"His argument is difficult to refute. Truth be told, I get the feeling that he is astoundingly well-versed in the Qur'an. Even Jaber bin Khayzran had to concur." Rihan answered, trying to assuage Turkan's anger, but it was no good.

"Why was he allowed to make his ruling in the first place? This is unacceptable! Unacceptable! Listen, Abu Abdel-Aziz, you must void his fatwa."

"My lady, I cannot. His argument has been accepted. No scholar can refute his extrapolation."

"Damn that wallowing interloper! I swear before Allah, I will make him pay a high price!" Turkan shouted; this time she did snatch up the golden goblet and hurl it at the wall, spraying red droplets of wine everywhere.

"My lady, why are you so determined to have Nouran Khatoun stay outside the Empire?"

Turkan spun towards the high judge and said tersely: "It is not your place to question me, only to carry out my orders!"

"Your pardon, my lady. I didn't mean..." Yahya started to stammer a reply, feeling he had overstepped his bounds.

"Abu Abdel-Aziz, you listen to me! Nouran and her son will be here in a few days. It is likely that this blow-hard will be with them so she can bring him before the Sultan so he can be rewarded for his deed. You will meet with him. You will find a way, as you usually do, to ensure *I* do not forswear *my* oath!"

"My lady..."

"Get out! I have no use for you until you have carried out your orders!"

Yahya bin Rihan was mortified by what the Sultan's mother had asked of him. She had subtly reminded him of what he had done to Qadi Wasil bin Ghilan a year before, and now she wanted him to do the same thing to this stranger.

(27)
Preliminaries

Even with what Yasimi had heard about the great city of Bukhara from Mohamed bin Ishaq Elbukhari, she never imagined it would be so vast, beautiful, and sprawling. Otrar was a mere village by comparison. Yasimi was entranced from the moment she saw an incredibly tall building towering over the high city walls. The merchant sheikh told her it was the minaret of the Jamia Mosque, the tallest – and grandest – minaret in the world.

"No city in the world holds a candle to Bukhara, my lady. Not in the fertility of the surrounding land, not in the beauty of its architecture, and not in the scholarship of its learned men or the genius of the people." The sheikh declared, clearly showing his pride, as the caravan approached the city walls that stretched out as far as the eye could see; they stretched nearly thirty miles and were about forty feet tall.

The caravan crossed through the first wall and was on its way to the second that divided the city center from the outskirts. The road was bordered by gardens and markets. There were buildings in the distance so large they had to be palaces, surrounded by other buildings made of brick. Jalal-Eddin's caravan was leading, and when it arrived at the gates of the inner wall, a crowd of city residents was there to greet it, led by Vizier Najm-Eddin Kablak who made his best effort to appear joyful at the arrival of the Emir and his mother. After exchanging greetings, they all – including Abdel-Rahman – went to the Sultan's palace where the Sultan himself was waiting for them in his chambers. Arrangements were made for the Mongol caravan to stay in the outer ring of the city once Emir Jalal-Eddin gave orders that they be accommodated in one of the palaces there. Princess Yasimi and the lead sheikh of the Mongol merchants would meet with Sultan Alaa-Eddin the following morning.

***

The Sultan welcomed his son and grandson first, hailing their safe return; he inquired about specific things that happened in Otrar during the trip. Eventually, he granted Abdel-Rahman entry into the chamber, also attended by Vizier Najm-Eddin and the High Qadi Yahya bin Rihan. The High Qadi felt very embarrassed in the Sultan's presence because he had been unable to uncover an Islamically justified way out of his oath made in passion, and this unknown stranger had – and no one even knew where the stranger gained his knowledge.

"Come forward, man, and kiss the ground between the feet of our lord the Sultan." The vizier commanded Abdel-Rahman when he saw the man had stopped some distance from the throne. "Hey, you! Did you not hear my command?"

Abdel-Rahman stayed where he was, ignoring Vizier Najm-Eddin Kablak. His attitude so enraged the vizier that he started towards Abdel-Rahman, intending to throw him to the floor at the Sultan's feet.

"Never mind, Najm-Eddin. Sheikh Abdel-Rahman is our guest, and we are in indebted to him and to his wisdom for saving myself and my family from embarrassment." The Sultan said, alleviating the dismay everyone in the chamber felt when Abdel-Rahman flouted protocol.

"State your desire, dear Sheikh; you will find us – with Allah's help – to be very generous."

"What I need, O Sultan, is not money nor temporary material possessions." Abdel-Rahman answered immediately.

"What is it that you need, then?" Sultan Alaa-Eddin asked, feeling confused.

"Maybe he wants courtesans, My lord." The Vizier said mocking him. Then he added under his voice to Yahya bin Rihan beside him, "I don't know how a nobody like this could have come up with something none of you could figure out."

The judge answered, "Maybe he just got lucky."

"Actually, I ask for a boy, Vizier." Abdel-Rahman said, looking at Najm-Eddin Kablak. Having left the Vizier stammering, he looked back to the Sultan. "Mohamed bin Mohamed Attousi, pupil of Qadi Wasil bin Ghilan – may Allah have mercy on his soul." He finished, explaining what he meant.

"How dare you!" the vizier started angrily, but he quickly regained control and looked to Sultan Alaa-Eddin who himself seemed angered by Abdel-Rahman's request and the mere mention of the name of Qadi Wasil bin Ghilan.

"And what business do you have with this heretic?"

Abdel-Rahman answered him with perfect composure, "The living have no business with the dead. My business is with his pupil, o Sultan." His calm irritated those present in the audience chamber even more, all but Jalal-Eddin and Mahmoud bin Mamdoud, who both supported Abdel-Rahman – though his odd request did catch them both by surprise and raise some doubts.

"If you will permit me, my lord…" the High Qadi looked to the Sultan waiting for a sign that he should continue.

"Let us hear what you would say, Abu Abdel-Aziz."

"Before Allah, I have mistrusted this man since I first saw him. Now he has shown us why and confirmed my concerns by making this request to free this boy, a disciple raised close to – and taught by – a heretic, the like of which this nation has never seen. The heretic's teachings forced my lord to do away with him and save the populace from his evil sedition. Wise men say, my lord: birds of a feather flock together, and crows will only join other crows. I believe this man is nothing more than a charlatan, come to take advantage of our good intentions. He has hidden himself behind a façade of wisdom and piety, but within he has come to spread poison among the ignorant masses."

"Ignorant is he who accuses people with no evidence, o Qadi." Abdel-Rahman answered Yahya bin Rihan, then continued, directing his words to the Sultan. "If the boy's offense is that he was a companion of Qadi Wasil bin Ghilan, then the High Qadi's offense is the greater for allowing a heretic, as he claims, to act as a qadi among the people. If the young man's offense was that he was born to Ismaili parents, then we should remember what Allah told us: No bearer of burdens should bear the burden of another. I swear to you, o Sultan, as soon as you release the boy, I will take him, and we will leave this land."

The high judge approached the Sultan and whispered to him, "My lord, do not let this suspicious character sway you with his honeyed words. I swear before Allah, I smell the odor of the heretic Wasil bin Ghilan upon him. Have him arrested, my lord. Let us examine what he believes."

"We find him blameless apart from his request for the pardon of a boy." Jalal-Eddin interrupted, then he went on, speaking to his father, "My lord, we do not want it rumored that the Sultan of the Khwarezmian Empire repays good with evil."

Alaa-Eddin nodded, indicating his agreement with his son's argument. The Sultan of the Great Khwarezmian Empire must be nothing less than generous.

"Very well. We have heard your request, o Abdel-Rahman. Had you asked for gold, or silver, or any of the pleasures of this world, we would have granted it to you as reward for your good deeds. Instead, you have asked that I pardon a boy of dubious status, which is another matter! I will grant you a second chance to make your request; make a better request that I may grant you a better reward."

"I have no need for greater joy in this world, o Sultan; I have all that I need."

"Very well, it is up to you. We have made the offer, you have refused."

The Sultan gestured permission for Abdel-Rahman to withdraw from his chamber, but Vizier Najm-Eddin objected.

"My lord, do not send him away without reward. This would give him the ability to create trouble for you among the people. They might say, 'look at this scholar who refused to accept compensation from the Sultan for his wisdom – see how he is different from the rest of the scholars in Khwarezm!'"

"Wait, you!" The Sultan called out, alarmed by his counselor's words, preventing Abdel-Rahman from leaving the chamber. "Would that you had not come to Bukhara and stayed where you were! However, as Jalal-Eddin has brought you here to me that I might reward you in some way, before Allah I shall not allow you to leave without hearing a request from you that I might fulfill – otherwise, I shall have you scourged for your disobedience to the rightful ruler!"

"Very well, o Sultan…"

"Say 'very well, my lord'!" the vizier cut in, stopping Abdel-Rahman short.

"O Vizier, my lord is also the Sultan's lord – and yours: The Merciful. Or do you have some other lord?"

"Stop this rubbish, both of you!" ordered the Sultan, losing what was left of his patience. "State your request, and we shall be glad to see the last of you!"

"It is said throughout every nation that the man has not been created who can best Sultan Alaa-Eddin at the game of chess." Abdel-Rahman said, pointing to the ivory chess set, laid out on a table next to the throne.

"If you are asking for this chessboard, it is yours."

"No, this is not my request."

"What then?! I swear, my patience with you has worn thin!"

"A grain of rice for each square on the board and let the number of grains be double the amount of the previous square."

The Sultan could not help but laugh as did everyone in the chamber. Even Emir Jalal-Eddin Manguberdi smiled at this strange request. Mahmoud bin Mamdoud was the only one filled with trepidation. "My lord!" he cried, "Do not grant this request!"

"It seems Mahmoud is afraid for his portion of the rice." The Sultan teased his grandson, then ordered his vizier to bring a bag of rice, unaware of the grave predicament just precipitated by the stranger.

***

From the moment Abdel-Rahman made the request, Mahmoud bin Mamdoud knew – based on his studies in mathematics – how dire the situation was. No matter how hard he tried to get his uncle's and grandfather's attention, though, neither would listen to a boy who had only come of age a year ago. Mahmoud knew that doubling the number of rice grains would reach quantities impossible to meet long before filling all sixty-four squares on the board; all the Khwarezmian Empire's reserves would not be enough!

The palace's quartermaster came with a bag of rice. Abdel-Rahman began counting out the grains, one by one, surrounded by the laughter of the Sultan and his courtiers.

"What a fool! The Sultan offers him all the best that life has to offer, and he asks for a handful of rice?"

Commentary along these lines could be heard from the vizier and the high judge. At the same time, Jalal-Eddin was visibly resentful, upset that the man who had saved his mother from the humiliation of being forced to stay outside the country was not suitably rewarded.

The rice grains doubled, from one to two, from two to four, then eight, sixteen, thirty-two, sixty-four, and finally 128 when the quartermaster finished the first row on the chessboard. The mood in the room remained light, still making fun of Abel Rahman, who now offered a small smile to Mahmoud, knowing that he, too, could see where this would end. In the middle of the second row, the mood started to shift; the number of grains now exceeded a thousand, and the whole thing was taking much longer than it should. That is when Jalal-Eddin, the Sultan and the attendees started to pay attention, noting that there were thousands of grains in the next square, which was only the fifteenth – would one bag of rice be enough?

"How many grains of rice are in a bag?" the Sultan asked his palace quartermaster, trying to hide the anxiety that was beginning to grow.

"I do not know, my lord. I've never counted them before." The old man answered. When he saw anger building on the Sultan's face at his answer, he quickly added, "but, my lord, seeing what we have counted so far and comparing that to what is left in the bag, I estimate there to be around forty thousand grains in a bag of rice."

"Will a single bag be enough, then?"

Everyone could see the answer to his question at this point.

"My lord, I do not think a single bag of rice will be enough to finish the second row of the chessboard, and we still have six more rows of squares."

At that moment, it was as though a curtain was lifted revealing the truth the audience had been ignorant of just a few minutes before, and everyone present understood the gravity of the situation – now a disaster!

With the beginning of the second row, they would have to use full bags of rice where they had been using grains, and that meant that by the third row they would need as many bags of rice as they were grains in a single bag! They would empty the palace's entire stock before they finished half of the chessboard.

The Sultan raged, "You tricked us, you foul deceiver!" in Abdel-Rahman's face.

"Surely the Sultan would not be fooled by one such as I. But you did make an oath to me that I must ask for a material reward. After you refused my first request, this is what I asked for and you approved. Where is the deception?"

The Sultan gestured for the high judge to come close to him, then he asked in a soft voice, "Is there a way out of this?"

Yahya bin Rihan hesitated a moment before saying, "You made an oath, my lord. You must grant him what he asked for or disavow yourself."

"Damn you, High Qadi! You leave me no options!"

"My lord, we will not be able to give him what he asked for, even if we gathered every grain of rice in the Empire!" the vizier said, explaining the scope of the problem.

"If you will permit me, my lord Sultan." Jalal-Eddin interrupted, loudly enough that Abdel-Rahman could hear. "From the moment I met this man in Otrar until we came to Bukhara, I have seen nothing but good. I think he is righteous and of high moral calibur." The Emir paused a moment, then turned to Abdel-Rahman, "If you would be so kind as to voluntarily rescind your request, we would be most grateful."

"Esteemed Emir, I thank you for your civil tongue and your kind words. I have no objection to rescinding my second request, provided the first is granted – the young man, Mohamed bin Mohamed Attousi."

"Damn you and that stupid boy! Damn this whole day!" the Sultan shouted, drawing his sword from its sheath. "If you don't get this vagabond out of my chamber this instant, I will take his head with this blade!"

"My lord!" Jalal-Eddin grabbed his father's arm trying to calm him. "Give the order to release the boy. Pardoning him will not harm you."

The Sultan slammed the sword back into its sheath, then stood a moment considering the situation. The room grew silent before he turned again to the high judge, "Release the boy! Be rid of him and the man who asked for him!"

Abdel-Rahman made no attempt to hide the small smile that found its way to his lips when his request was granted. He looked to his right and – without moving his lips and without anyone hearing him, the way he usually did when speaking to Murad – he said, "The preliminaries are over now. It will not be long before the main journey begins!"

(28)
The Favored Grandchild

Ghiyath-Eddin, the Sultan's youngest son, returned from his alleged hunting trip when he got news of what had happened in Otrar and the ruination of the careful plot he set up with his grandmother, Turkan Khatoun, and her brother Yanal Khan. With Jalal-Eddin accompanying his mother outside the Khwarezmian Empire into Mongol territory, they had a golden opportunity to be rid of him. Otrar's governor's men could do the deed with their own blades and the Mongols would bear the blame. This would eliminate the greatest obstacle between him and the throne yet leave his hands clean. This was a unique opportunity; the Sultan's anger with his wife, his oath that he would force her to camp outside the Empire, both coming at a time when Khwarezm was at war with the Abbasids and their allies, the Saljuks and the Ayyubids to the west. This left no safe option for Nouran Khatoun and her son Jalal-Eddin but to go east. It was an impeccable plan and would have worked perfectly if it weren't for the unexpected appearance of the man called Abdel-Rahman.

Upon his arrival in Bukhara, Ghiyath-Eddin went straight to his grandmother's palace where she awaited him so they could discuss what options remained open to them. Especially considering the additional complication of the Sultan's pending proclamation that Jalal-Eddin would be the crown prince — which could come at any moment, despite Turkan's objections.

"Where did that damned man come from?! By Allah, my blade thirsts for his blood!"

"You must be deliberate, and not as quick to act as your father. What happened, happened. We must find some way to keep Alaa-Eddin from naming his crown prince. In doing so, we will buy ourselves time to find another way to get rid of Jalal-Eddin Manguberdi."

"Time is running out, grandmother. These opportunities don't grow on trees."

"True, the opportunity may not present itself. That's why we must seek one out, or create one ourselves, if needs be."

Before he asked "How?", Turkan could clearly see Ghiyath's lack of comprehension. She smiled broadly and took her grandson's face in her hands, "You are like your father and his father before him. You are a straightforward warrior, good with sword and spear, but reason and deliberation are not your strong suits. Fear not, leave it to me. For now, I want you to go to Alaa-Eddin's chambers and attend his meeting with the sheikh of the Mongol caravan's merchants. I have received word from my brother that one of the Mongol Khan's granddaughters is with him, and that he brings a letter from the Khan to your father."

"The Mongol Khan's granddaughter? Why would he send her to us?"

"Because he wants an alliance with the Khwarezmian Sultan. He wants to take us over through marriage rather than invading with warriors."

"What?! Allah knows that my father would never permit an alliance with those unbelieving savages!" he shouted, overcome by fervor.

"You have much to learn, angry idiot boy! I want you to listen to me and do what I say is best. The Mongol culture is not all that different from the Turkic tribes; they both spring from the same root. The Mongol Khan sent his closest female relative of marriable age so she can marry the closest male relative of the Sultan of Khwarezm."

"Jalal-Eddin!"

"Very good! You've started to use your mind. I know my son well. His response will be the same as yours a moment ago – he will refuse the alliance and the girl will go back to her grandfather. This is where your part comes in, Ghiyath-Eddin. You will convince your father that sending the girl back would be a grave insult to the Mongol Khan and could cause him to declare war on us. We are already in a conflict with the Abbasids to the west, the last thing we want is another war on our eastern border. That said, it would be best for all to marry the girl to Jalal-Eddin!"

"But Jalal-Eddin would never accept this sort of marriage." Ghiyath-Eddin said, amazed at what his grandmother was saying.

"That is exactly what I am counting on. I want Jalal-Eddin to refuse to follow the orders of his father the Sultan!"

(29)
Reflections

Murad was experiencing a state of calm that he had not felt in a long time. It didn't seem as though his disembodied life caused him the kind of stress that was the norm for him not so long ago. Quite the opposite, being unfettered from the needs of his body and his appetites was freeing. It granted him a sort of mental clarity that he had never experienced before. What was strange was that he had been so frantic, but when he surrendered to this new situation, he discovered a level of self control he had never felt or seen in anyone before. Every minute detail of the events around him fit with the others like pieces of a puzzle, gradually coming together to reveal the whole picture. The amazing part of it all was that as he witnessed the course of events and really considered what he saw, his memories of these things, originally just a jumbled mess, took shape and became organized in the way memories ought to be. This created another dilemma, however, making it more difficult to uncover the meaning of what was beginning to reveal itself to him. How could a human being have more than one memory? Or, to put it more accurately, how could a human remember multiple things happening at exactly the same moment? How could he have been in Jeddah and Riyadh at the same time? How could he have an affair with Sarah Alquwit, and not have one at the same time? How could Hadeel both know him and not know him? These puzzles took on even greater depth as they approached his memories of things that had hindered him before, especially when he remembered that Tunisian waiter he had found dead. Something had been drawing him to that dark-skinned, thin young man – Mohamed. It seemed like everything was somehow connected to him. The headache that intensified in the last phase of his corporeal life, especially when he got close to Mohamed. *I saw him before, but the circumstances were different. It was some other time, some other place... but where? How?* Murad felt like the answer to these two questions would clarify many of the other things he needed to understand in order to place last pieces of the puzzle. Knowing those answers would let him see the truth that he was still miles from understanding. He didn't despair, though, because some things, simple things in the scope of the questions storming around in his head, were starting to become clear. Events were still unfolding, however. The more he saw the things that the strange man was setting in motion, the more he was able to place them within an amazing pattern. He thought Abdel-Rahman's presence here at this time was of great significance, and in some way, Murad felt connected to the greater pattern of everything that was happening. All he had to do was watch and *see* in order to spot the truth.

"Which one of these two lives do you prefer to live? Which of the two Murads do you want to be? The oppressor, or the oppressed? The one exiled for a sin he didn't commit, or the one who speaks before everyone, lover of the wife of a man of means? The humiliated, or the one who can humiliate everyone?" Abdel-Rahman asked him on the way to the cell where Mohamed bin Mohamed Attousi was being held.

"Are these the only two options I have? I can be a scared little mouse, or a wolf stalking sheep? Surely there must be a third option! There must be!"

"And if there isn't?"

Murad Qutuz took a moment to consider the question, then answered with a determination he'd never felt before: "If there isn't, then I'll make one."

(30)
The Triangle of Oppression

"**A** body can be bound and thrown into the worst prison, but a free mind cannot be restrained or imprisoned. A free mind can pass through walls; it cannot be subjugated by tyranny!" Mohamed Attousi repeated this to himself over and over in his cell in the dungeon under the Bukhara citadel. This was something his teacher, the judge Wasil bin Ghilan, said often – and these were his final words before they crucified him.

Whenever Mohamed Attousi remembered how they tortured his teacher and the slow, terrible death he suffered, he honored bin Ghilan and prayed for him. He had only been with him for a few years, but that time was full to overflowing and rich with learning. Mohamed had never seen or heard of a man as intelligent as Wasil bin Ghilan, or one with as much knowledge, not in the past nor in the present. Bin Ghilan never stopped seeking knowledge, and he followed a path that carried him to the ends of the earth. More than any of this, the judge loved righteous action and despised evil and oppression; he was never afraid to speak the truth despite curses and threats from an unjust sultan. People had forgotten all of this – or perhaps they were made to forget. Either way, the result was the same; they wanted him to be both corrupt and a source of corruption, whether he was or not, and so, as far as the people were concerned, he was. *They are sheep shorn of independent will.* Every time the young man remembered how they threw garbage at his teacher as he hung on the cross, he withdrew and sought refuge in his faith. *They described him in the most hideous terms for no reason other than to please their masters.* Each time he remembered the sight of him dying under the burning sun in the center of Bukhara, how they cut out his tongue and threw it to a pack of stray dogs to eat; every time he thought of this ending, his mind would carry him back to the beginning: *Allah be praised, but how capable people are of living in denial!*

The young man remembered how it started for him. Wasil bin Ghilan came to Tous, returning from a research journey that carried him to cities in Iraq, the Levant, Morocco, and Andalusia, and finally Mecca before he started back. He had stopped in Tous for supplies as he traveled the road to Bukhara when he saw Youhna the Scribe, from Karkh, near Baghdad, leading people astray by debating the scholars of Tous about Jesus and the Qur'an. He asked the people about the Qur'an and if they believed it to be God's words; he asked if it was ancient or contemporary. When the people said it was ancient, he asked about Jesus; "Was he not the word of God given to Mary?" When they answered in the affirmative, Youhna would ask:

"Then why do you consider the words of your Lord ancient, and the word he gave to Mary contemporary?

Does the single form not have the same features as the plural? Reason then dictates that Jesus, son of Mary, is ancient, because he is the Word of God. You assert that God's words are ancient and could not be a more recent creation because this would contradict the fact that they come from ancient time and there is nothing ancient in this way apart from God. Therefore, Jesus is God!"

They could not come up with a convincing counterargument. The people's scholars failed them, until Wasil bin Ghilan entered the city and heard these debates and the trouble they had caused. Bin Ghilan asked to debate Youhna the Scribe.

Youhna began by asking about the nature of the Qur'an. Wasil told him it was Allah's words given to His messenger. Youhna then asked if these words were ancient or if they were a more recent creation. Ghilan's response was that the knowledge contained in them was ancient, but their form was created more recently. Youhna was not ready for this answer; it invalidated his next question concerning Jesus, so he tried to disparage Wasil's view by saying it was not the view of the body of Muslims who spoke of the ancient nature of the Qur'an. Wasil cut off further argument in this vein by providing proof of other Islamic scholars who agreed with this statement, prominent scholars like Abu Hanifa Al-Nuaman and Ali bin Al-Madini as well as Imam Bukhari, from his own city, who had gathered a collection of true Hadith and was evicted from Bukhara for saying that the form of the Qur'an was created.

Youhna the Scribe faded into obscurity, the strife he caused dissipated, because he was not equal to Wasil bin Ghilan whose reputation grew after this debate. The governor of Tous honored him and kept him close until Ghilan's trial.

Mohamed Attousi saw that debate when he was just a child of twelve. He was amazed by Wasil's great knowledge and his strong arguments. Though he has been raised by parents who followed the Ismaili sect, he was different from his peers and questioned and argued about everything. This earned him the censure of his teachers who simply wanted to teach what they had been taught in turn. They were not interested in digging for the truth Mohamed was looking for through his constant arguments and defenses. In Wasil bin Ghilan, Mohamed found a better teacher, just as Wasil found Mohamed to be the best pupil in Tous, and a good companion when he returned to Bukhara the following year.

By then, he had been away from the great city for almost fifteen years, time he spent sojourning in various countries as well as the year he spent as a judge in Tous. He was welcomed warmly by the people who remembered how he had been while studying in one of the Grand Mosque's circles. The High Qadi, Yahya bin Rihan, was glad to see him as well; they had spent many sessions learning together in the Sultan's presence before he left on his journey. However, the Wasil bin Ghilan who returned to Bukhara was not the same man who left all those years before. (Mohamed Attousi remembered one of his teacher's sayings: "If knowledge does not change you, then make the effort to change it.") Wasil had learned much over the course of his voyage, adding to the broad understanding he enjoyed before he left. He had changed gradually over time.

"One day, my boy, miracles will become an everyday occurrence. Do you know when this will happen? When people discover the laws of the universe. This is no impossible goal. Knowledge of the Book gave Asif ibn Barkhiya the ability to approach the throne of Bilquis before the Prophet Suleiman, peace be upon him, could blink. The manifest Book of Allah resides in the laws of the universe."

What bin Ghilan believed, he would not hide from his disciple. The search for the laws of the universe was the greatest goal of mankind; through these laws, they would find a deeper understanding of the Lord and better see the wonder of His creation. This knowledge is what Allah taught to Adam, enabling him to become the greatest of Allah's creatures, such that even the angels honor mankind with Allah's permission. This opinion has many repercussions, one of which brought about Qadi Wasil bin Ghilan's suffering.

"I know, Mohamed, that one expression of how just Allah is can be seen in how he made human beings able to make themselves more valuable through study. The more people learn, the more capable they are to shape their own futures. This is one of the ways the Almighty honored the children of Adam above all creatures. This is how we have been stewards of this trust. He entrusted us with the ability to choose."

But the same humanity that Allah honored, a portion of whom put their trust in Wasil bin Ghilan, is the same humanity that denied rights to others, oppressed them, and cast them aside. *People are so evil and oppressive.* Mohamed Attousi sat in his shackles, in his prison cell, remembering the death of his teacher. *Coercion is the creed of the evil ruler, used as a collar around the necks of the populace.* The young man remembered how a simple idea can cause the originator to suffer after it shook the thrones of tyrants who dominated their people in the name of religion, working through a handful of priests whose only duty was to legitimize the tyrant's oppression and to control the minds of the public and rabble. The Triangle of Oppression, Wasil used to call it. It's three sides are the ruler, the priesthood, and masses. He believed that the most evil side of the triangle was the priest legislator, represented in the Caliphate and the Empire by some of the government's qadis. What Mohamed had seen, however, made him believe something else: He believed that the most evil of the three was the populace. The masses accepted their humiliation, they cheered for those who cheated them, and cut off the hands of anyone who tried to free them from their bondage. *Damn the ignorant masses! Damn the populace that slays their savior, woe to them and their willful ignorance! Damn the public whose evil is no less than the one who oppresses them!* The young man's heart broke every time he remembered how everyone abandoned his teacher based on the mere rumor that the Sultan was angry with him, and how quickly they turned against him when High Qadi Abu Abdel-Aziz Yahya Rihan issued a fatwa claiming Wasil was corrupt, followed by the most horrendous sentence: death by crucifixion.

***

"O Allah, wisest of rulers, greatest in knowledge. O Lord, You created this universe and established its laws for the righteous, and You created its wonders and secrets for all who seek. I ask You by all Your names to grant me the wisdom I need to distinguish falsehood from truth, the courage to speak the truth, and the strength to support myself and all those who walk the path of truth."

Mohamed Attousi repeated this prayer that he learned from his teacher, who, in turn, had learned from a man he met years ago during his journey to Mecca. When Mohamed asked about the man, his teacher simply said that he was the wisest man on earth – and he never spoke another word on the subject. The young man recited this prayer each morning and any time he felt under stress – more often now that his teacher had been struck down. He knew very well that the word "truth" was the thing that landed him in this dark, desolate cell in the dungeon under the Bukhara citadel. Had he said what they told him to say, his fate would have been very different. That's why Mohamed felt the need to recite this prayer over and over, particularly after the prison guards claimed that in all the years they had served, they had never seen a single person leave Bukhara's dungeon once they had been put there.

"You are here to stay, boy! You might as well get used to your new home."

One of the guards even jokingly told him he should beg the Sultan's mercy to allow him to join his teacher in the afterlife.

Much of his first year in prison was spent in reflection and thought, recalling everything he had learned from his teacher. He clung to hope. Every time he saw signs that his hope was fading, he would immediately recite the prayer bin Ghilan had taught him. This was how the young man had carried on until the unexpected moment came, when the guard who had never seen a prisoner leave the dungeon came to tell him that a man named Abdel-Rahman had come with a writ from the Sultan, ordering his release.

(31)

Across Lands

Things unfolded just as Turkan Khatoun expected they would. Ghiyath-Eddin walked the path she set out for him, placing himself between his father and his half-brother Jalal-Eddin Manguberdi. Mohamed bin Ishaq Elbukhari, sheikh of the Mongol caravan's merchants, showed Genghis Khan's letter to the Sultan; it was an offer of trade between the two lands and for stronger ties based on the marriage of his granddaughter Yasimi to whomever Sultan Alaa-Eddin chose from among his sons. Ghiyath-Eddin, with support from Vizier Najm-Eddin Kablak, convinced his father that this union was in the best interest of the empire, and that Jalal-Eddin, as the eldest son, was the most appropriate choice to marry Genghis Khan's granddaughter. At first, the Sultan was not convinced that he needed an alliance with a Mongol king who was nothing more than a tribal warlord, a barbarian from the eastern steppes – even if he was King of China and had conquered his enemies, the Karakhatta, who had plagued Khwarezm since the time of his father with wars that waged until just a few years earlier. But his vizier convinced him that it was in his best interest to secure the eastern border of the empire until they had defeated the Abbasids in the west and laid claim to Baghdad. A political marriage would make Genghis Khan an ally, one who could help in the western campaigns; it was this that convinced the Sultan to order the marriage that Turkan Khatoun knew Jalal-Eddin would never accept, even if doing so meant his father would cut him off. Marriage to the Mongol king's granddaughter would be a harsh blow to his wife, Shirin Alghouri, sister to the last sultan of Ghazni, that stubborn nation to the south that had resisted the Khwarezmian advance until Sultan Alaa-Eddin broke its power after long effort, and put his son in place as governor there. The Emir still had a lot of trouble to deal with until one of the supporters of Ghazni advised him to marry Emira Shirin, telling him that doing so would gain the favor of the remaining Ghorids and their allies because once he had, the Ghorids would become his own men and warriors through marriage. Jalal-Eddin tried to explain to his father that marrying Genghis Khan's granddaughter would anger the Gaznians and bring them trouble throughout Afghan territory, but his arguments only angered the Sultan to the point where all he could see in his oldest son's words was disobedience to his orders. At that tense moment, Ghiyath-Eddin intervened, as instructed by his grandmother, and offered to marry Genghis Khan's granddaughter himself as a means of salvaging the situation. This made him look like the righteous son whose only desire was to do whatever is best for the country and to obey the Sultan's orders – the child most worthy to be crowned prince.

***

Meanwhile, in Otrar, Akrama and the rest of the Mongol merchants found themselves in an unexpected conundrum. They discovered that governor Yanal Khan coveted the goods they carried; when Vizier Khalid bin Mansour invited them to his palace, then at the end of the evening he told them that if they wanted to do as the governor desires, in order to extend their welcome in Otrar, gateway to markets throughout Khwarezm to them, they would have to demonstrate greater goodwill and respect. When they asked what he meant, particularly since they had been sending boxes full of all kinds of luxurious goods to the governor from the first day, the vizier told them it wasn't enough. He told them that a clever merchant would not worry about losing a single caravan in order to be able to bring more caravans in the future. That's when Akrama figured out what he meant, and he would not accept such cheap blackmail. He was furious, and shouted in Khalid's face to tell "Yanal Chok" (knowing it to be a nickname the governor hated and that none dared use it in his presence or in the presence of one of his men) that the Mongol merchants were protected by the Great Khan, and no one, no matter who it was, could blackmail them and deprive them of their trade.

The next day Yanal Khan received a report on the conversation between his vizier and the Mongol merchants – and the news spread throughout Otrar that Akrama the merchant had called the governor Yanal

Chok. Combined, these tales fanned the flames of Yanal Khan's rage against "the evil men" who dared stand against him. Without hesitation, he issued an arrest warrant for the Mongol merchants and the confiscation of all their possessions, followed by their public beheading. *Let them be an example to any who dared cross the governor of Otrar, Yanal Khan.*

* * *

Some thousands of miles to the east in Karakorum, Hudhayfah bin Samaan looked around himself, surprised to learn that this collection of tents was Genghis Khan's capitol, a man whose chain of victories over China and the kingdom of Karakhatta had reached the ears of the Caliph Annasser Li-Dinillah Ahmed bin Al-Hassan in Baghdad. What he saw before him was not even the equal of the smallest village in Muslim territory. For a moment, Hudhayfah thought his guide must have gotten them lost, but that idea was quickly dispelled when the guide spoke to a group of horsemen who had come out to meet them. They all turned towards him and let him know through gestures that to see Genghis Khan, he must first give them his sword and dagger, then he should go to the tent pitched on a small hillock. The only thing that set this tent apart from the rest in the camp was its location. He tried to ask his guide if he needed to meet a doorman or vizier before entering the tent of the Mongol king, but the Tatar horseman told him that the khans of the steppes know nothing of doormen, and their tents were open to all; particularly to one who brings a letter from one of the world's kings.

Hudhayfah felt some trepidation at entering Genghis Khan's tent without his Tatar guide, but the man refused to stay with him, explaining that he had completed the job for which bin Samaan had hired him by bringing him to Karakorum safely. He worried about how he could explain the contents of the letter he brought from the Muslim Caliph for Genghis Khan without his guide who had also been serving as interpreter, particularly since Hudhayfah did not speak this nation's tongue.

"Peace be upon the messenger of the Muslim Caliph in Baghdad." A man said in Persian-accented Arabic, greeting Hudhayfah, who had not expected to find anyone in the Mongol King's tent who could speak his language.

"And peace be upon you. How did you know who I am? No one here knows my business other than the guide, who I am almost certain did not reach this tent before I did – neither him nor any of the warriors who spoke to him."

Despite the astonishment clearly visible in Hudhayfah's demeanor, the man did not offer an answer to his question. Instead, the Persian invited him to sit and introduced himself as Abdallah bin Othman Alkharsani, one of Genghis Khan's viziers. It wasn't until the vizier pointed him out that Hudhayfah knew which of the men present was Genghis Khan. He was sitting on the ground like everyone else. The sheepskin tent was supported by two upright poles, and none of the opulence and wealth he was accustomed to in Baghdad was on display. *These are the people who overcame the armies of China and Karakhatta? I swear, if only the Caliph could see what I see before me, he would rethink sending me to these people!*

"My Master, Commander of the Faithful, Shadow of Allah on Earth, Protector of Religious Fervor, Caliph Annasser Li-Diniallah wishes you peace, sends you this letter and awaits your reply that I might bear it to him as quickly as possible."

Hudhayfah withdrew the letter, bearing the Caliph's seal, from his robe and handed it to Genghis Khan. The Khan handed it in turn to Abdallah so he could translate its content.

The letter contained the Caliph's permission for the Mongols to attack the Khwarezmians. In fact, it all but encouraged them to do so, and promised Genghis Khan that he could keep all the land he took from Alaa-Eddin Mohamed Khwarezmshah. The only condition was that they should go no further than Khorasan. The Caliph declared his willingness to coordinate with the Khan so the Mongols could attack from the east and his army attack Khwarezm from the west at the same time, and the letter also promised Genghis Khan a handsome reward if he brought the head of Alaa-Eddin to him.

Abdallah had only just finished translating the contents of the letter when Genghis Khan stood, rage coloring his features, and addressed his vizier in firm tones: "He says to the messenger that he should tell his leader that Genghis Khan does not wait upon the permission of any human being to attack any location. Tell him also that we have a treaty with the Sultan of Khwarezm, and we do not break treaties."

***

Turkan Khatoun waited until Jalal-Eddin Manguberdi left Bukhara in a rage, headed back to Ghazni, before she went to the Sultan to fulfill the promise she made to her dearest grandson Ghiyath-Eddin, that she would protect him from the marriage he only pretended to approve of in order to curry favor with his father, moving that much closer to being named crown prince.

"The Mongol Khan sent his granddaughter, not one of his daughters. How could he expect the Sultan of Khwarezm to marry her to one of his sons?"

"What are you trying to say, mother? That we should send her back to him?" the Sultan asked, then looked at his vizier who had remained silent.

"No. No, don't send her back. You should marry her to a grandson, not one of your sons." Painting a sly smile on her face, Turkan Khatoun looked at Nouran who was sitting on a couch near her grandson Mahmoud bin Mamdoud. She continued, "Maybe Mahmoud would be best for such a marriage."

When Nouran heard her grandson's name suggested, she jumped to her feet, "You have no business with Mahmoud, he is only a boy!"

"A boy?" Turkan countered, "At his age, his grandfather was leading armies!"

"My lord, if you will allow me, what my lady Turkan Khatoun has proposed is precisely the right solution." Vizier Najm-Eddin Kablak added in support of the Sultan's mother.

Nouran tried to respond to them, but the Sultan raised his hand, indicating that she should not speak. "Mahmoud is no longer a boy. It is time for him to bear some responsibility as befits any member of this family."

With this declaration, Sultan Alaa-Eddin Mohamed made up his mind. The granddaughter of the Mongol Khan should marry none other than the grandson of the Sultan of Khwarezm, not one of his sons.

(32)

Moussa's Inn

I t was several days after his release before Mohamed Attousi met the man who secured his release after nearly a year in prison. His second appearance was no less sudden and unexpected than his first, after he left him in a room rented at Moussa's Inn. The young man spent the whole time in his rented room, never going out, not even for food; he only went out to meet natures requirements. One of the servants brought him food each morning and evening. He passed the first five days and nights in this manner, until he started to think he had traded his old cell for one much cleaner, with fewer rats, and better food.

Living in the room gave him time to think about the man who introduced himself by a single name – no family name or place attribution – just Abdel-Rahman, an old friend of his teacher the Qadi Wasil bin Ghilan. That's all he got as they crossed the distance between the dungeon and the inn situated in Bukhara's outer ring near the great wall. He had remained virtually chained to the inn for the last several days, as his new master had requested after giving Moussa, the inn's owner, a pouch with enough dinars to cover the room's rent and the cost of food and drink for several days.

The man seemed strange; Mohamed started to think. Did he owe something to his old friend that he wanted to make up for by freeing his disciple from prison, where he had been sent for refusing to give false testimony against his teacher? Mohamed had been punished for refusing to slander Wasil bin Ghilan; they wanted him to say his teacher lusted after young men and had sex with them. However, he quickly dismissed the idea. How could his new master know about these things when they took place in a closed room between himself and the high judge, Yahya bin Rihan. Certainly, the judge would not have told anyone what he had asked Mohamed to do. The corruptor would never give himself away! On the few occasions where he ran into the inn's owner, Mohamed tried to learn more about Abdel-Rahman. He quickly found that the man knew no more than he did; Moussa, too, had never met him before, nor had he heard anything about him other than bits of gossip here and there from patrons who had been in Otrar.

"No doubt, he is a stranger here." Moussa added at the end.

Mohamed had no other choice but to wait at the inn until Abdel-Rahman came as he promised. Boredom took root after waiting several days alone in his room; he felt like he was still a prisoner. He decided to go down to the dining hall, full of people coming from all over to order food and drink. There he could learn something about what had happened during the last year from listening to people talk.

Taxes had gone up, he found, and prices, too. The rich got richer just as the poor got poorer. He wanted to ask them: *What's new about that? Didn't you accept this humiliation?* But he stayed silent.

The Mongol caravan was also the subject of discussion; it had come to Bukhara with all kinds of goods from China. The thing that caught his ear, however, was that the granddaughter of Genghis Khan had come with the caravan. Later, he heard some others talking about Emir Jalal-Eddin's sudden departure, only a few days after he arrived in Bukhara in the company of the Mongol caravan. These were the current events that most of the patrons were talking about, though they didn't understand and weren't curious about the details. Mohamed Attousi, though, was able to piece together a logical picture of the course of events based on the small facts people talked about, as his teacher had instructed him.

"These are mathematical equations, similar to algebra: the given facts lead to the results. Initial facts lead to conclusions. Logic rules over all aspects of life. Use all your senses, my boy, as they were created to be used. Use your mind as it was intended to be used."

This was the most important lesson he learned from Wasil bin Ghilan. How to listen and watch, and how to see the truth. "All truths, no matter how small, no matter how great, must obey the laws that govern everything. If you learn the laws, the truths will be revealed, and miracles explained."

Even so, though some facts about current events in Bukhara were revealed to Mohamed Attousi based on what he heard in the inn and saw from the state of the people there, one important thing remained beyond his comprehension. It bothered him through the days that had passed since he left the prison: who is this stranger named Abdel-Rahman?

***

"I hope you have recovered somewhat?"

Mohamed looked to his right and saw Abdel-Rahman standing there, seemingly having appeared out of nowhere, moving silently as a cat.

"I feel better, thanks be to Allah and to you, master." The young man answered timidly, then invited his sponsor to sit, hoping to hear something from him that would reveal a bit of who he was.

"Do you see that young man standing by the entrance?" Abdel-Rahman asked, indicating a Circassian man who had just entered the inn. He was looking around, like he was trying to find someone. Abdel-Rahman went on, "I think he's looking for us, to have us come and speak to his mistress who waits outside."

Mohamed looked at the youth, then at Abdel-Rahman in undisguised amazement. "How do you know?"

"Look closely. Tell me what you see."

"I see a young Circassian-looking man, no older than twenty, maybe a bit younger, turning his head this way and that like he is looking for someone."

As Mohamed finished his sentence, the young man noticed them. After looking at them for a few moments, he started moving in their direction. When he approached, he timidly asked, "Pardon me, master. Are you Sheikh Abdel-Rahman?"

"Who is asking?"

"There is someone who would like to speak to you and this young man outside."

"Tell your mistress that we will be out directly."

The Circassian stammered, not knowing what to say, astounded that the man had known his master was a woman waiting outside. How did he know? Did he see her without being spotted himself? No less astounded was Mohamed bin Mohamed Attousi who sat perplexed by the whole situation.

"How did you know about him and his mistress?" he asked as soon as the young man withdrew.

"I looked at him. There was a youth with Circassian features, nearing the end of his teen years. He had thick hair but a smooth face, and he was dressed like someone from Bukhara. He stopped near the door without coming in, then began looking around, and he seemed worried. This is what we both looked at, but I saw what you did not."

Mohamed considered the description Abdel-Rahman gave. The details matched the facts, and everything seemed clear now. He started blaming himself. *How did I not notice that? How did I not see?*

"A young Circassian man in Bukhara, wearing the same clothing as the locals, is not with a delegation that as come for some temporary reason like trade. He must live here. He is nearly twenty years old, yet he had no beard or moustache and the hair on his head is thick and full; this description fits one who was castrated very young. Therefore, he must be a Circassian personal slave; and that sort of slave works in the home of a woman of high status. What would bring him to the inn? Did he come to eat or have a drink? The fact that he stopped by the door without coming in, despite there being open tables, means that he did not come to sit. Instead, he was looking for someone. His eyes covered the whole place, but he kept looking because he did not see us at first — we are in the corner furthest from the door. So, he must have been looking for you and me. When he approached us and told us there was someone outside who wanted to talk to us, who could it have been other than a mistress who did not wish to enter an inn full of men?" Mohamed was pleased with his explanation, though it had come to him a little late. His only consolation was that it was better to see it late than not to have seen it at all.

***

Abdel-Rahman exited Moussa's Inn with Mohamed Attousi. Together they walked towards a fine carriage parked a short distance away. The young Circassian was standing next to it, and when he saw the man and the youth walking towards him, he immediately turned to inform his mistress through the window of the carriage.

Nouran knew quite well that coming here was dangerous, particularly when the eyes of Turkan were always watching her. If her mother-in-law knew what she was planning, she would immediately inform Sultan Alaa-Eddin – she would accuse Nouran of treason and disloyalty. Despite the danger, Nouran was deeply convinced that this was what she had to do. This was the least she could do in memory of the only man she had loved with every fiber of her being, the man who should have been her husband if things had gone differently.

Lu'lu opened the carriage door for his mistress' two guests, allowing them to enter. Once they were inside, he began patrolling the area watching for anything that might threaten their safety, and for the city watch who were spread throughout Bukhara. Despite his efforts, this task was not one of his usual skills. He was willing to do anything his mistress asked of him; he grew up in her service, having been brought to her as a child from the Caucasus following one of Sultan Alaa-Eddin's invasions. Many had lost their lives, and some lost their freedom and a few, like him, had lost their manhood.

When Nouran looked at Mohamed Attousi as he entered the carriage with Abdel-Rahman, her eyes filled at the memory of how she had been unable to do anything to rescue his teacher. The urge to burst into tears nearly overcame her, but she managed to rally her control at the last second, avoiding wasting time with useless mourning. She knew that she could not remain in this place for long if she wanted to avoid tipping her hand.

"Peace and the blessings and mercy of Allah be upon you." Abdel-Rahman began.

"And to you, worthy scholar and wise man. I still owe you a great deal, I don't believe that I could repay you no matter what I do. However, I have come to warn you and the lad; maybe this will give some measure of payment towards my debt."

"Warn us about what?" Mohamed asked in shock, interrupting the Sultan's wife.

She finally turned to look at the young man whom she had tried to avoid looking at from the first, afraid she might lose control over herself. Nouran did not want tears to fall where they could see. But when he spoke, and when she looked at his face, so full of defiance and curiosity, memories of his teacher's entire life, from childhood to death, filled her. Despite her best efforts, she couldn't maintain her composure.

"Allah knows! Allah knows I tried to talk him out of staying in Bukhara! I told him what would happen to him, but he wouldn't listen. He was so stubborn! If he had just listened to me and left when I warned him, he wouldn't... Wasil bin Ghilan didn't deserve what happened to him. It wasn't right! I knew him from when he was a child, he loved righteousness and always sought after the truth. He was one of my father's students, his favorite in fact. He liked him so much that, when he saw I loved Wasil, he set up our engagement. Allah's will overruled over my father's, though, and he died before we could be married. My uncle would not honor my father's promise and he nullified the engagement. Instead, he married me to the man who was crown prince at that time, Alaa-Eddin Mohamed, because that served his own purposes. Wasil couldn't handle staying in Bukhara, so he left. He wandered all over the world, not returning for years. When he came back the first time, he did not stay long before setting out once again. He was gone for a number of years this time as well. He repeated this pattern several times, until the end."

Nouran burst into tears again, remembering how Wasil bin Ghilan had been harmed. She regained her composure and went on. "The things he said displeased a lot of people. They lay in wait for him, watching for the right moment, when he started talking about human desires and the ability of humankind to choose their own fate, denying the doctrine of determinism. I heard Yahya bin Rihan warn the Sultan about the consequences of this kind of talk spreading among the people. I tried to convince Alaa-Eddin that it would be enough to exile him, but the high judge wanted more; so he went to the head of the snake: Turkan! He knew perfectly well that the Sultan could refuse her nothing. She convinced him! She was the one who convinced the Sultan that exile would not be enough to quell his teachings. She convinced him exile would make him a hero! No, they had to impugn his religious standing and his morals before ordering his crucifixion so the people would despise him! Doing so would set an example for others who might consider following in his footsteps. I pray Allah's mercy for you, my beloved, you did not deserve this affliction!"

Abdel-Rahman stayed silent, moved by Nouran's tale. Mohamed Attousi was silent as well, though tears soaked his thin moustache. He had no desire to interrupt her, he simply wished to hear everything she was willing to say.

"When I heard you had been released from prison, I offered my praises to Allah." She continued, addressing the lad, "but neither the Sultan nor the High Qadi wanted to see you freed. That's why I had my servant Lu'lu stay near Alaa-Eddin and tell me if he heard any ill plans regarding the two of you. This morning he told me something that sounded suspicious. A warrior from Otrar came, sent by Yanal Khan, to tell the Sultan that the Mongol merchants were nothing more than agents sent by Genghis Khan to spy on the Khwarezmian Empire and to spread corruption within!"

(33)

Ignorance...
Powerlessness

Murad Qutuz immediately saw the importance of Nouran's warning. It wasn't just about the Mongol merchants; it encompassed everyone who came with them including Abdel-Rahman and Yasimi! For some reason, Murad's worry wasn't for Abdel-Rahman or the young man he had worked to free from prison; it was for the young girl, mature beyond her years, he felt so much affection for. She and the others now stood accused of espionage. At the very least, she was in for some harsh treatment as punishment for the charges against her grandfather Genghis Khan. Either way, there would be no marriage; instead she might be thrown in prison as punishment! Murad felt like he had to do something, to go find her in Bukhara and warn her. But how? He had just started moving down the street when he remembered his condition. How could he warn her when Abdel-Rahman was the only person in this place and time who could hear him? How could he warn her as an incorporeal shade, much less do anything else? Murad decided to go back to Abdel-Rahman, at least *he* could warn Yasimi. That's when he heard his voice calling him:

"Forget about the girl for now, there is something more important!"

Abdel-Rahman was nowhere to be seen, but his voice could still reach Murad, who had thought he was accustomed to all the surprises his companion had to offer, despite how closely he played things.

"What? If we don't help her, something bad will happen to her. Didn't you hear what Nouran said about her husband's ruthlessness?" Murad shouted in desperation.

"If you care about the girl's affairs, you are on your own. Otherwise, let her follow the path she is travelling."

Murad paused to really consider the matter. What should he do? If Abdel-Rahman didn't care about Yasimi, why should he? Especially given that this wasn't his world. Murad didn't belong in the here and now. How would he benefit from helping a Mongol girl whose people would soon bring great tragedy and destruction on the Muslims of this time? A voice inside started to encourage him to return to Abdel-Rahman and forget about the girl, he had had nothing in common with her anyway. Murad Qutuz hesitated for a moment, then started back towards Moussa's Inn to rejoin Abdel-Rahman and their new companion, Mohamed Attousi. As soon as he did, however, his vision shifted back to a time he immediately recognized. He saw himself at the gas station, a group of young men punching and kicking the Bengali worker. He saw himself take a few steps towards helping the poor man, then he saw himself retreat. Next, he saw their meeting the next day. This vision only lasted a few moments before he came back to where he had been.

***

As she had been doing since arriving in Bukhara, Yasimi went for a walk alone through the city streets and alleys, ignoring warnings from Mohamed bin Ishaq about the men who came to this city from all over, some of whom might harm her. Having been raised in Genghis Khan's orbit, Yasimi didn't feel like she needed anyone to protect her; she was perfectly capable of protecting herself. She would tell the sheikh, "Who would dare attack a Mongol princess, much less the granddaughter of Genghis Khan?" his only choice was to acquiesce to her stubborn insistence.

"In a few days, you will be the wife of the Khwarezmian Sultan's grandson. This will require you to behave in accordance to the customs of the royal family." Bin Ishaq told her that day, but Yasimi wouldn't listen.

"Did my grandfather send me to marry a man or to marry their customs and traditions? I am a free woman, and I will remain a free woman! The Khwarezmians will have to learn that Mongol women are not handmaidens; they give birth to the greatest warriors in the world! When they are born, their first cries fill the people with terror!"

Mohamed bin Ishaq had observed this wild girl's birth, he had watched her blossom into an extremely beautiful and intelligent young woman, the equal of any Mongol warrior her age in courage and skill. As much as he loved

211

her, he pitied young Mahmoud bin Mamdoud – the boy would never be able to tame her. She was like a wild mare; she would only be broken by the firm hand of a strong warrior with a powerful presence and deep commitment, one who demands her respect through his firm control and great skill; not a young boy who was still learning at his grandmother's knee.

Yasimi went on wandering through Bukhara, ignoring the odd looks some people gave her, especially those who had never seen a girl from the Mongol lands before, wearing clothing that resembled men's clothes, and instead of earrings and trinkets, her only ornament was the dagger at her waist. Despite her strange appearance, no one caused her any harm. If some made comments, she simply ignored them. That kind of person was below notice, not worth looking at, much less responding to, though she was more than capable of dealing with the situation and silencing them had she wished. However, she had come out to see as much of this great city as she could. Its shops, buildings, and alleyways were so different from anything she had ever seen before. She had read about such civilizations and the variety of their landmarks before, but the reality was so much more; it was overwhelming. *What an enormous city! Karakorum is nothing compared to Bukhara; it is like a barn for their animals in comparison!*

Her wanderings took her near the citadel on the northern heights, overlooking the whole city. This was what she had seen several days before from outside Bukhara. She examined the tall building for a while before noticing some soldiers were looking in her direction and whispering, like they were talking about her. At first, Yasimi didn't pay much heed; they were probably bemused by her appearance like everybody else. It didn't take her long to see that there was something much more dangerous afoot. Some distance away, she saw a group of Bukara's soldiers leading several merchants from her grandfather's caravan, chained together like slaves. Yasimi stood in disbelief as she watched this strange scene unfold before her eyes. She didn't understand what was happening until she saw an open cart loaded with the blood-drenched bodies of the caravan's guards! *What happened?!* There was no clear answer to this question, and Yasimi found she had no desire to stay where she was in order to get one from the soldiers. When she saw the men who had been looking in her direction start rapidly towards her, she turned to run, only to find herself surrounded by another group of soldiers.

***

Murad had to do something! He refused to stand there with his hands bound. He refused to simply observe, unable to influence or take part. He kept roaming the streets of Bukhara, looking for the house where Yasimi was staying, though he didn't know where it was. This random search was better than doing nothing, better than feeling powerless, as far as he was concerned. At that moment, loping through the streets and alleys, he wished he could go where he wanted to by simply wanting it, even if he didn't know where it was. He wished that not knowing about something could be removed as an obstacle to making it happen. For a moment he wondered which was worse: ability paired with ignorance, or powerlessness paired with knowledge. Murad didn't try to answer this question, though. He was preoccupied with something that seemed to him as the end of a thread that might lead him to what he desired. He noticed several soldiers on horseback moving like they were in a hurry. *Are they on their way to arrest Yasimi and the Mongol merchants?* It seemed so; Murad had to follow – though he had no idea what he would do when he got to Yasimi.

The soldiers headed in the direction of a large house in the southern district of Bukhara situated between the inner and outer walls of the city where the Mongol caravan guards had been allowed to store their weapons when they accompanied Jalal-Eddin several days before. Their weapons did them no good on this day. They did not sense the spears the Khwarezmian soldiers aimed at their chests until they had already pierced their bodies, turning them in to a heap of corpses next to the walls of the house they were guarding. Murad saw the solders shoving his way through the door one of the merchants had opened to investigate the shouts he heard outside. That poor man was the first one they arrested and shackled. The soldiers quickly dragged the others from the house; they were all clearly distraught, unable to believe what was happening to them. One of them was shouting, cursing the Khwarezmian soldiers and calling them all sorts of names, especially once he saw the bodies of the Mongol guards on the ground. His shouting and bluster brought him nothing but a blow from one of the soldiers, hard enough to knock him flat, prostrate on the ground next to one of the corpses.

"Where are the rest?" the commander asked.

That's when Murad noticed that Yasimi wasn't in the house. Mohamed bin Ishaq wasn't with them either. *There is still time to warn her, then. Maybe she'll be able to escape!* Once again, Murad thought about how he could get to her, or to the sheikh in charge of the Mongol caravan's merchants who might be with her. Time was slipping away, and the soldiers would sweep the city searching for her. He had to come up with something, otherwise...

As these thoughts coursed through Murad's mind, he saw something he hadn't thought he would see again, particularly in broad daylight in Bukhara. It had been weeks since he saw it last, when it killed the Mongol warrior outside Otrar. He saw it again now, but this time it was headed for him. As it came, it took on a featureless body, but a face that was very familiar. For a moment, he thought this strange creature was trying to look like him!

Murad tried to leave, to go back to the inn where he might find some help from Abdel-Rahman as he fled from this phantasmagoric creature. Even though he did not know what it was, he did know it was dangerous. Just as he turned towards the inn, a part of the city he knew, at least, he found the creature was in front of him, behind him, and on both sides; it had him completely surrounded and closed in on him leaving no room for movement. In that moment, Murad Qutuz realized – for the first time since he found himself in this disembodied state, far from the world he knew – that he was not safe, even if he was a spirit with no body.

(34)
Light and Darkness

"Murad, Murad, Murad... What am I going to do with you? You insist on interfering in things that are none of your concern. It's like you are trying to get me to punish you! You must know, my dear, that my patience with you has its limits." The phantasm said in a voice meant only for Murad who was astonished by what he saw before him and around him.

"What... what are you talking about?"

"I'm talking about your constant attempts to be the hero, or whatever. You aren't good enough for that. How do your people say it? You're meddlesome.

"I love these expressive terms. Why don't you learn from the people around you and just leave things be? Look where your thoughtless behavior has brought you. You need to be concerned with how you can get back to your wonderful life, the one you left behind. How will you ever get back to the way things were before you started doubting your life and the people around you? Listen closely, my dear Murad. I won't keep you long. Leave Yasimi be. Whatever happens to her, it isn't your business."

"You speak to me as though you know me. Who are you? *What* are you?" Murad asked, amazed at what he heard.

"Me? I'll just say that I am closer to you than you think. I wouldn't be exaggerating if I said I was your best friend, the guardian who watches over his friend's interests. If you only knew what I did for you before you threw yourself into the mouth of the volcano... I gave you the two things that everyone in your world searches for and enjoys the most — money and sex! But what can I say? The appetites of men will only ever be filled by the soil of the grave."

"You gave me? Are you... did you send me here?" Murad's desire to know the truth began to outweigh his fear of this being, though he had seen its capacity to cause harm the first time he met it.

"No, I am not responsible for all this. But I can help you. If you want me to."

"You can help me? Really?"

"Of course. I will help you get back to your time. After all, what concern is this time, this ancient history, of yours? I will teach you the things your friend Abdel-Rahman has been keeping from you."

"You know Abdel-Rahman?"

"Yes, I know him well, though I wish I didn't. He is full of lies; you shouldn't trust him!"

"Alright, let's go! Help me get back."

"Hold on, dear one, we have to come to an agreement first."

"On what?" Murad asked.

"Let me show you."

With that utterance, the scene around them shifted to one Murad immediately recognized. It was the palace of the governor of Otrar. He saw the governor, furious when his vizier brought him the news of what had passed between himself and the Mongol merchants. Murad heard the governor give orders to kill them all and seize their goods. The vizier tried to dissuade him from doing this, warning that it could bring suffering on the whole country, but Yanal Khan wouldn't listen. Murad could see the rage in the governor's eyes, it was paired with greed and the two were feeding on one another. His view shifted to the next day, after the merchants were killed. The vizier asked the governor how he would justify his actions when the Sultan learned of what happened. No easy answer presented itself to him, so the vizier suggested that he claim the merchants were spies, arrested as they roused the people against the government; that was why the governor had them executed. Now the scene shifted again to the present in Bukhara, but this time his view was near the citadel where Yasimi had been headed, not knowing what had happened to her companions a few moments before. Murad again felt the overwhelming urge to do something to help her, to warn her about what was going to happen.

"Look at that idiot girl." The entity said sourly. "Ignorantly walking to her prison. Do you know why, Murad? Because it is her fate, written in stone, and you naïvely want to keep her from it!"

The scene continued to unfold. Yasimi saw the soldiers leading the captured merchants to the citadel and some of the soldiers noticed the Mongol girl they were searching for. The men surrounded her just as she started to retreat.

"If you want my help, you must first forget about this girl. You must not try to interfere in things that do not concern you. You must back away, Murad, just as you did at the gas station."

He had to let it go. That's all he needed to do, and everything would go back to the way it was before. He would return to his world, his body, his life! All he had to do was back away, just as he had at the gas station, and let Yasimi's fate be what it would be – and what concern was it of his? He didn't even actually know her, and what was there to know? She was just a Mongol girl, offspring of the beasts whose savagery against Muslims was well documented. Was it not they who would destroy cities and slaughter people? That's what he remembered from the history books he had studied in school. Yasimi was no more than another fruit from that poison tree; he should leave her to her fate and back down. *Yes, let me walk away from this! Just as I did at the gas station...*

But something inside wouldn't let him, and it was strong this time. A strange feeling, one he couldn't explain, kept him from obeying the creature's request. It was the same feeling that made him look for Mohamed, the Tunisian waiter, at Ghanim Elsaaidi's palace. Suddenly, without meaning to and without even knowing how, Murad found himself radiating a bright light that rapidly intensified, a flash that filled the black phantasm, which would have broken up and vanished had it not withdrawn from how it surrounded Murad and held him in place. The creature was not the only thing effected by the flash. Murad could see that the soldiers surrounding Yasimi crumpled to their knees, placing their hands over their eyes as though suffering great pain. Yasimi, though, was looking at him with eyes round and filled with awe as though she… could she see him? For a moment, Murad thought she did. For the first time since he found himself in this situation, he could see himself! He could see his limbs! He had incarnated, even if it was just for a moment, even if he didn't know how!

Before the flash faded, the entity was able to gather its strength and it looked furious! Something like a black whip emerged from it and wrapped itself around Murad, cutting him off from everything around him. It seemed to Murad like he was trapped in a dark, narrow casket with only a sliver of light visible.

"I warned you, but you wouldn't listen! I told you not to cross me. Damn you! Now I will show you the price of your foolish actions. I will wipe you out of existence! I will send you to hell where you belong!"

As it finished speaking, there was another flash, brighter and stronger than the one a moment before. This time, though, Murad wasn't the origin. The entity spun towards the source of the flash. When it saw the cause, it was filled with desperate panic that made it lose its grip on Murad. It left in an instant, having seen power it did not possess.

(35)
Memories of Bukhara

Three decades had passed since Mohamed bin Ishaq Albukahri left the city he was born and raised in, the city he had dearly loved, the same city that he felt had betrayed him. More than that; it had conspired against him and done him evil: his mother had kicked him out, her husband had taken what was rightfully his, and no one from his family stood up for him.

Is it Bukhara that has changed or is it just me? he asked himself over and over as he went to the house that had been his father's house and had been stolen from him. It had been several days since his arrival in Bukhara and he found the buildings even more beautiful than they were in his memory; the walls were thicker and taller, and the elite of the city were wealthier as well. He was still asking himself the same question as he rallied his courage and went to face the past he had tried to forget during his years away. *How can a man forget when present events continually conspire to remind him of the past?*

The house didn't seem empty. He saw a little girl open the door for the milk seller crying his wares to the morning. She was a pale girl, no more than nine years old, her features hinting at Sindhi origins; she must have been taken during one of Khwarezm's wars with the Ghorids to the south.

"May Allah grant you a good morning, little one. Is this the home of Isha…" he didn't finish his sentence; this had not been his father's house for a long time. "My apologies. Is this the home of Othman bin Sanjar?" he felt a twinge in his heart when he uttered the name of his mother's husband, calling it that man's house when it was his rightful inheritance. That's when he realized that this was why he had put off this visit.

"Yes, this is his house. But my master has been out since dawn and will not return before sunset."

Mohamed bin Ishaq smiled then, he wanted to tell the little girl that he had not come to meet with her thieving master, which would require him to shake the man's sinful hand and look upon his despised countenance.

"That's alright. I am here to see your mistress. Please tell her that Mohamed bin Ishaq has returned."

"Mohamed bin Ishaq? Does she know you, or are you related to her?"

"Yes, I believe I am."

"Pardon me sir, I did not know. I am new here."

The girl led the guest into the house and asked him to wait in the sitting room while she informed the mistress that he had come. Before she went, she remembered the jar she was carrying and asked if he would like a glass of milk. Mohamed thanked her and asked for her name before taking a dinar from his pocket and giving it to her, a move that caused her such excitement she nearly dropped the jar.

Some time passed before the door to the sitting room opened, admitting a young man in his late teens. From his features, Mohamed could tell he must be a child of Othman bin Sanjar.

"Peace be upon you." The youth offered in a tone that held no welcome for the stranger.

"And peace, Allah's mercy and blessings be upon you." He answered, completing the greeting as he examined the person who was likely his half-brother.

"The serving girl told us you are inquiring about my mother. Who might you be?"

"I am Mohamed bin Ishaq. I'm sure your mother told you about me." Mohamed answered, walking up to the lad, ready to accompany him into the house.

"Mohamed bin Ishaq? Where does my mother know you from that she would tell me about you?" The boy asked, beginning to get angry with this blustering visitor.

"I am your brother, your mother's son."

"My brother?"

"Yes, from her first husband, Ishaq bin Abi Alhassan."

"Are you crazy, man? You claim that my mother married your father, yet she is younger than you! More than that, my mother didn't marry anyone before she married my father!"

This unanticipated response gave Mohamed pause. Did Othman marry another woman in addition to his mother? "I beg your pardon, but is your mother not Aisha, daughter of Ahmed Elkharaz?"

"No, she is the sister to High Qadi Yahya bin Rihan!"

Mohamed was quite embarrassed at the error he had made, however... "Could you tell me about my mother? Your father's first wife?"

"I don't know anything about that! I think you have overstayed your welcome, and this visit is over." The boy said, clearly not wanting to say anything further. He gestured for this burdensome guest to leave his house.

Mohamed left the house that had been his birthright, his mind spinning. Had his mother died? This was one of the things he was afraid he might be confronted with; coming here and finding his mother was not there, that death had reached her before he did, before he could kiss her head and tell her that he had never forgotten about her, before he could ask forgiveness for staying away from her for so long. He knew deep down that his mother, though she had kicked him out of the house, still loved him, and that her cruelty had been no more than a wisp of summer cloud. He cursed himself for being gone for so many long years, for this estrangement that never should have been.

"Mohamed? Is that you?" The voice came from a shop on the street corner. A man of an age with Mohamed came out, "I didn't believe my eyes when I first spotted you coming down the street! But I knew it was you when I saw you headed for your father's house. Oh my god, it really is you! Where have you been all this time, man?"

Bin Ishaq recognized him and returned the shopkeeper's embrace; how could he forget his neighbor and childhood friend, his constant playmate in the streets of Bukhara.

"Ali! How are you, my friend?" His joy at seeing his old friend was somewhat tempered by what he had learned. Ali noticed the slight reticence, and he knew what was behind it, but did not want to speak of such things before bringing Mohamed to his home. This sort of thing should not be discussed on the side of the road.

***

Mohamed bin Ishaq wished he had never come back to Bukhara, that he had stayed far away to the east, never to hear how his mother suffered under debilitating pain. Human capacity for cruelty and brutality was boundless, but stranger still was their ability to condone and justify it.

From his friend Ali, the merchant sheikh learned how Othman bin Sanjar had divorced his mother and kicked her out of the house just a few years after Mohamed left Bukhara. When his mother went to Qadi Yahya bin Rihan to protest the divorce, accusing her husband of embezzlement and fraud, the judge sentenced her to flogging for libel. When she tried to force her way into her house, which Othman had stolen from her, after he had married the judge's sister, the judge sent her to prison. There Mohamed's mother remained, imprisoned in the Bukhara citadel, for more than a year before the Lord took her, freeing her from the punishment she suffered.

Mohamed fervently wished to leave the city. It was no longer his home, it had become something else entirely, something he couldn't recognize anymore. It was full of contradictions. On the surface, it was beautiful and rich, but inside it was hideous and poor. The men appeared to be godly and righteous, but they were filled with greed and corruption! As he walked back to where they were staying on the other side of the city, he looked at his surroundings. No more could he see the beauty he left some thirty years before. What he saw was a disease-ridden city that needed to be burned to the ground so it could be reborn, pure.

He walked through Bukhara's streets, but instead of going to the vast house where he was staying with Yasimi and the rest of the merchants, he found himself near the citadel on the south side of the city where his mother had died. He barely had the chance to take another step when he saw a group of Khwarezmian soldiers leading his companions in shackles, their clothing disheveled, injuries visible as clear indications that they had been harshly beaten. At first, he couldn't believe his eyes; he wanted to get closer – but a hand grasped him from behind and kept him from moving.

"If you go out there, they will take you, too, and you will share their fate." A voice said behind him, seeming to have appeared out of nowhere.

"What's going on? Why are they in shackles? Where are the soldiers taking them?" bin Ishaq asked, in shock at what he was seeing.

"To the citadel where they will be imprisoned and tortured to death." Abdel-Rahman told him calmly. He told the sheikh what had happened to his companions in Otrar, and how Yanal Khan and sent word to the Sultan that the Mongol merchants were spies for Genghis Khan, and that was why they had been arrested.

"I have to see Sultan Alaa-Eddin! I have to tell him the governor of Otrar lied!"

"It's no use. The Sultan will not take your word over his uncle's."

Something important occurred to Mohamed then, "What about Yasimi? Where is she? Have you seen her?"

Abdel-Rahman took Mohamed by the shoulders and looked into his eyes before telling him firmly, "You cannot do anything for her now. You cannot help her if you get arrested. They will figure out that you aren't with the people they are bringing to the citadel at any moment. When that happens, they will seal all the city gates. Every member of the city watch, and every soldier here will scour the city until they find and arrest you. This is your one opportunity to get away. Go to Moussa's Inn. You'll find a horse waiting for you there. Take it and go – but do not go north or east. If you do, they'll catch up to you and capture you. Head south, for Ghazni. Hide out there for a day or two. They will not look for you there, where you are still in their territory. Gather the provisions and supplies you need, then head for Karakorum."

"But what about Yasimi?"

"As I said, you can do her no good if they arrest you. Leave her to her fate; it may be that Allah will guide her to the best path." With that, he turned away from Mohamed bin Ishaq, looking back towards the citadel when he saw a flash of light. Mohamed turned to look as well. A few moments later, another flash came, brighter than the one before, that knocked him to the ground and nearly left him blind. It was only moments before his sight returned and the merchant sheikh gathered himself together and turned to check on Abdel-Rahman, but the man was nowhere to be found. He had vanished just as suddenly as he had appeared.

(36)

A Difficult Path Towards the Truth

"That thing! It nearly... it almost killed me!" Murad kept repeating, unable to believe what just happened, then a question occurred to him, "Was it a djinn?"

"No, it wasn't a djinn. It was something far more dangerous." Abdel-Rahman said with his usual calm, though he was starting to show some signs of weariness, which came as a surprise to Murad – he'd never seen Abdel-Rahman tired before.

"More dangerous than a djinn? What in the world is it?"

"Knowledge provided at the wrong time can increase ignorance. You will know when it is time for you to know. The thing you need to get into your head right now is that you are not ready yet to get involved in the things you are witnessing. Do not think you can simply shift from one state to its opposite any time you feel like it. Things aren't that stable – that ability requires skill, and skill requires control."

Abdel-Rahman fell silent for a time, thinking. Then he whispered a question, as though he were speaking to himself, "but why Yasimi?"

At the mention of her name, Murad looked at the Mongol princess. He saw the soldiers leading her into the citadel after they recovered from the flash of light that stole their vision. It was like nothing had even happened. Yasimi was not acting like her usual self, she wasn't struggling at all. She went with them, meek and scared.

"Will you leave her to be imprisoned? What has she done to deserve this fate?" Murad shouted, once again wanting to go to her, to do something – anything – to help her.

"He who does not learn from his mistakes is doomed to repeat them." Abdel-Rahman said, keeping Murad from moving in her direction. "For the present, she has nothing to fear. There is someone else who needs our help more right now, and time is running out. We have to get moving."

Abdel-Rahman immediately took off, headed east. Hesitantly at first, Murad followed, finally accepting what Abdel-Rahman told him. It was easier once he calmed down a little. As they went, he started to review what had happened to him just now, trying to understand something. He examined those moments several times until he blurted out, "I think she saw me!"

Abdel-Rahman stopped suddenly. For the first time in his experience with the man, Murad could see his normally neutral face showing surprise. "Explain what you just said."

"Before you came to rescue me, and when... I don't know what I did... I caused that flash or spark or whatever it was... I don't know how to describe it. For a moment I saw my body materialize, and at the same time I saw Yasimi looking in my direction — and she got scared. I'm almost certain she saw me, what's more, she seemed to recognize me. I don't know how it could be, but that's how it seemed. The strange thing was that some of the soldiers were blinded by whatever it was I did, but none of them saw me. Maybe they'll chalk the flash up to the sun glinting off some reflective surface, but not Yasimi."

Abdel-Rahman stood where he was, thinking about what Murad told him. He started walking quickly again, still in the same direction, without saying a word.

***

Moussa knew how risky it was to do what he was doing. But he also knew that the greater the risk, the greater the reward. That's what he thought when Abdel-Rahman offered him three times the value of his horse to get it ready immediately for a friend, a man called Mohamed bin Ishaq, who he said would be coming soon to take it. Moussa had his suspicions about the whole thing. He knew no one would pay triple the cost of a thing unless they were in great need, and who needed a horse more than someone needing to flee? *That's alright, let him run if he wants to run, so long as he pays for it — and for my silence!* Everything always has a price. This wouldn't be the only risk that Abdel-Rahman wanted to pay for; there was something much more dangerous ahead. Moussa knew about it, and he had seen the purse full of diamonds the stranger offered; even though it might destroy him. The greater the risk, though, the greater the reward – and what a reward! If he had that, he would be one of the richest men in the city, and he wouldn't need to work ever again. If he lived to enjoy it, that is.

"He's late." Moussa told Mohamed Attousi who was starting to worry as he waited for Abdel-Rahman. Attousi had brought three horses to a paddock near Bukhara's eastern gate. Moussa thought about leaving, just going back to his inn where he could watch the madness that they were about to get into, but visions of those glittering diamonds he saw before agreeing to be a part of this adventure made him wait.

"Here he comes." Mohamed pointed to Abdel-Rahman, then mounted his horse. Moussa did the same.

"Just a moment." Abdel-Rahman said as he checked all three horses. "Not yet. We have to wait for a bit."

"What are we waiting for? Is there someone else coming with us? You only asked me for three horses!" The tension was getting to Moussa, he was visibly shaking with fear. The high, clear sound of a horn heard throughout the city punctuated his words. Though he had not heard this horn sounded for a long time, he knew exactly what it meant. *The gates of Bukhara are to be closed, no one is to be allowed in or out of the city!*

"Let's go. Now."

Abdel-Rahman had his horse set off in the direction of the eastern gate with Mohamed close behind and Moussa, hoping none of the soldiers in the vicinity recognized him. The great gates were swinging closed when the captain of the guard saw the three horses headed straight for it. He called out to his soldiers to prepare their spears; his orders had been clear: "No one leaves the city alive until we capture the last three!"

Moussa was terrified. He was starting to berate himself for agreeing to this insane adventure that could only end in destruction. For a second, he thought about turning his horse around and going back into the city, leaving Abdel-Rahman and Mahmoud. What value was there in wealth if he wasn't alive to enjoy it? He could still withdraw, especially if none of the soldiers recognized him as the third rider. He could go back now, and no one would come looking for him. They would look for Mohamed bin Ishaq instead, who got scared when he saw them gathering at the eastern gate and fled back into the city... that's what they would think. Moussa looked around, *It's now or never!* The gate was nearly closed, and once it was, they would not be able to leave Bukhara, even if they managed to survive past the soldiers' spears. At the very moment he decided to turn back and break his agreement with Abdel-Rahman to go to the wall, Moussa saw something unexpected. The gate stopped moving, like something was blocking it, leaving just enough of a gap for them to slip through – if they could get past the spears! Then he saw Abdel-Rahman, riding the first horse, pull two small pouches from his pocket, then he withdrew a small pointed stick. He stroked it with his fingernail, and it started burning. He touched it to thin ropes that trailed out of both purses, then threw them at the soldiers. They produced a thud and more smoke than he had ever seen in his life! The soldiers were tossed to the ground by the explosion, and some of them had superficial wounds, but most were simply terrified by the thick smoke coming from the two pouches tossed by the stranger in the green turban.

At that moment, as he passed easily through the gate, Moussa started asking himself if he should be afraid of the soldiers, or if it was wiser for him to fear the sorcerer who had just pulled a genie from his pocket?!

***

After half a day of running, the horses were completely blown. Abdel-Rahman and his two companions stopped near a quiet village near Bukhara. He took a pouch out of his leather pack that looked very similar to the two he had thrown at the Khwarezmian soldiers at Bukhara's eastern gate. He gave it to Moussa, who was terrified when he first saw it, the memory of the soldiers still fresh in his mind. He dropped the pouch, and a few diamonds slipped out.

"You've fulfilled your contract with us, and now we have given you what we promised. I think it would be best for you to break away from us now before any of Bukhara's soldiers catch up."

Moussa barely heard what Abdel-Rahman said, his vision was filled with the diamonds. His fear was erased; he was too full of avarice. He jumped down from his horse and started gathering the stones off the ground.

"Thank you, sir! Thank you very much! You are too generous! I'm your servant forever!" he continued offering his profuse gratitude as he examined the diamonds. He couldn't believe the vast treasure he held in his hands, more than he ever dreamed of! More than enough to renovate the inn if he wanted, though he would never need to work again.

Abdel-Rahman and Mohamed entered the town after saying goodbye to their third companion. They found an inn, deserted apart from the owner who welcomed them warmly because the place had not seen a visitor in several days.

"What was it you threw at the soldiers? It looked like saltpeter, but I've never seen smoke like that from such a small amount!" Mohamed asked after the inn's proprietor went to get them food and drink. His excitement came through in the question, he hadn't known his companion was an alchemist.

"It was just a mixture of saltpeter, powdered charcoal, and sulfur." Abdel-Rahman told him.

"Powdered charcoal and sulfur." Mohamed repeated as he considered it, then he asked another question, "Where did you learn to make this strange compound?"

"It isn't all that strange. It has been known among the scholars of China for centuries."

"Have you been to China?"

"To China and many other lands, seeking knowledge." Abdel-Rahman answered.

Mohamed nodded, satisfied by the answers to his questions. Then he started to look around, examining the inn, before noticing something that made him curious. "Is it wise for us to come to a place like this empty inn? The proprietor is sure to remember us if any of Bukhari's soldiers come, which they probably will as they follow our trail."

Abdel-Rahman didn't answer the lad's question, he just looked at him, indifferently.

"Aren't you worried they'll catch us and..." Mohamed didn't bother to finish the question; he could see the answer in his companion's expression. "You *want* them to follow us. Everything we have done was just to give the merchant a chance to escape. But you aren't done with Bukhara yet?"

"Listen son, you don't owe me anything. You are welcome to go now. There is a pack on your horse containing everything you need. If you leave now, they will not catch you, I promise."

Mohamed Attousi smiled and said, "No... I'll stay with you. Not because you freed me from prison – Allah knows I did not consider myself a prisoner when I was captive in the bowels of that damned citadel and bound with shackles. My mind was free, and no high judge, no sultan could chain that down. I pitied those outside the prison who thought themselves free, not knowing that they were prisoners to their fears, their hypocrisy, and their threadbare beliefs. I will stay with you because I have no desire to lose another teacher after I lost Qadi Wasil bin Ghilan. If I have learned anything in my young and simple life, it is that there is no harder path for a person to follow than the one that leads to an understanding of the truth."

(37)

Warlock

Though Sultan Alaa-Eddin Mohamed did not know how much he could believe Yanal Khan's claim that the merchants in the Mongol caravan were spies sent by Genghis Khan, and though he was not happy at how quickly the governor had killed those in Otrar, there was one thing he knew: he had to go along with his uncle if he didn't want to earn the ire of his mother and the entire Kankali clan – which made up a full third of his army including his senior commanders and advisors. The Sultan also thought of something that he had missed at first: by accusing the Mongols of espionage, he would have the excuse he needed to discredit Abdel-Rahman who embarrassed him in front of his courtiers; Abdel-Rahman had come in company with the merchants, which meant he was one of them. Still, there was the issue of Genghis Khan himself, and what to do about him after what had happened, and what to do with his granddaughter, whom he had sent in order to gain a treaty by marriage.

"My lord, as the Mongol King has shown us hostility, I see no reason to marry his granddaughter to your grandson, Emir Mahmoud bin Mamdoud. Instead, you should give her to one of your commanders as a serving girl." Najm-Eddin Kablak advised the Sultan after breaking the news that Abdel-Rahman and Mohamed Attousi were imprisoned at the Bukhara citadel, and that a hundred of Khwarezm's best warriors were on the trail of Mohamed bin Ishaq, and they would certainly capture him.

"Is it permissible for us to enslave a girl who came to us with peaceful intent, especially after we have already announced we would marry her to our grandson?" the Sultan asked, not wanting it to be said that he did not keep his oaths.

"This is a simple matter, my lord. We can ask the high judge to issue a fatwa for us that shows the Mongol Khan's actions amount to an act of war. Then we have the right to enslave his granddaughter; at that point it would be illogical to have an emir from the ruling house of Khwarezm marry a Mongol serving girl."

"Just right, Najm-Eddin, you shrewd vizier!" The Sultan did not hide his admiration for the advice his vizier gave him. Unlike Turkan Khatoun, who burst into the chamber without warning.

"O, you imbecilic man!" The Sultan's mother shouted, unconcerned by who might hear her voice outside the chamber.

"Mother!"

"Yes, he is an imbecile, advising you to do the wrong thing. If he had an ounce of sense, such a thing would never have crossed his lips."

"My lady Turkan Khatoun, what have I said that has brought your censure?" Vizier Najm-Eddin tried his best not to show the anger at the insult she had just hurled at him, though deep inside he wanted to draw his dagger to cut out the tongue of that vulgar woman.

"The granddaughter of the Mongol Khan must marry Mahmoud! Especially now that you have lost the sheikh of the Mongol merchants. It is only a matter of weeks before he returns to his Khan and informs him of what happened to the rest of the merchants – and the warriors who had accompanied the caravan."

"It will not come to this, my lady. Our best warriors are pursuing him. They will certainly capture him before he leaves the country."

"Didn't I tell you that you're an idiot? That warlock who calls himself Abdel-Rahman has fooled you again! He got you to follow him after he made a scene. This gave his companion the chance to flee in a different direction!"

"Impossible, my lady. The soldiers saw three riders flee through the eastern gate."

"But you only captured two – Abdel-Rahman and the boy. Why was the merchant sheikh not with them?"

The vizier fell silent, not answering her question; he started to see what Turkan Khatoun was driving at.

"Allow me to answer, then, vizier. He was not with them because he exited through a different gate. The third man your soldiers saw was someone they hired to make you think they all went out in the same direction!"

The Sultan looked to the vizier who looked completely embarrassed and couldn't speak. He looked back to his mother. "How do you know that this is what happened?"

"Because it is what I would have done if I wanted to ensure someone other than myself would escape and survive. My son, you must learn to think like your enemies if you hope to defeat them!"

"Damn that bastard! He *is* a warlock; I felt the corruption in him the moment I laid eyes on him." The Sultan shouted, filled with wrath at the man who had fooled him yet again in plain view of all.

"He certainly is a warlock, my lord. He cast the ashes of the djinn he uses at the soldiers as he escaped! If it hadn't been for that, he couldn't have gotten past our best men; we would have caught him there at the eastern gate and learned that the merchant sheikh was not with them."

"We must behead him tomorrow before all Bukhara for this!"

"No." Turkhan Khatoun interrupted her son. "Death would be too easy for him. People like that do not deserve easy. Let him suffer a few weeks in the depths of the prison without food, both him and the boy, then have them both crucified for their execution."

"What of the girl, mother? Why are you determined that she should marry Mahmoud? I don't think a pact with the Mongol Khan will be any good after all this."

"Quite the opposite. If you marry the Mongol Khan's granddaughter to Mahmoud, he will think twice before doing us any harm. Who will he consider more important? His granddaughter, blood of his blood, or a bunch of Muslim merchants who do not share his faith and are not members of his tribe?"

Sultan Alaa-Eddin Mohamed smiled then, convinced that his mother was right. He looked to his vizier who simply nodded in agreement. Despite Najm-Eddin's hatred for that shrewd woman, all he could do at that moment was thank God she was a member of his own tribe; if she were not, he would have no way to protect himself from her worst machinations.

(38)

Darkness and Light

Fear, confusion, loneliness... did she have to remain a captive to these feelings, no matter how she tried or how hard she struggled to free herself from them? Was it her fate to continue fighting against Tabtinkar's curse through her whole life, even here in Bukhara? Wasn't it enough that she left everything behind in Karakorum, everyone who loved her, and everyone she loved? Yasimi never imagined that she would end up in a place like this, imprisoned within the citadel of this rich city. She believed she was alone. Confusion over the situation crashed over her in waves, and fear began to seep into her heart. Confusion, because she still didn't know the truth or where she might find it. Fear, because she knew the extent of her confusion and that there was no one who could help her.

On that day when she mistakenly entered Tabtinkar's tent, she thought that fate had led her there to show her the truth, to reveal the world ruled by the god of light and the god of darkness. One god who produced only good, and one who produced only evil. Abdel-Rahman destroyed her faith in a single conversation, then abandoned her when she needed someone like him to teach her and help her find her way out. There was nothing worse than for a person to be imprisoned in their mind and imprisoned physically at the same time, unless it was being ignorant of the cause and had no idea where to start looking for an answer. Who could she ask about the thing she saw outside the citadel a few days before? Who could explain that light she saw emanating from the same creature whose shadow she saw in Tabtinkar's tent? Offered a choice between remaining a prisoner in this terrible dungeon and understanding what happened in Karakorum and here in Bukhara, she would rather understand – even if it meant spending the rest of her life in the bowels of this place. But it seemed to her that her fate was to be imprisoned in body and mind.

***

Something inside Yasimi had broken on the day she was shackled and brought to the citadel along with the rest of the caravan's merchants. That's what she sensed, and the feeling of being broken bothered her. She had always hoped to be like her grandmother, Borte, who had taught her and cared for her more than her mother had. Yasimi had hoped to have her strength, her determination, and her resolve – she had been kidnapped, then fled, and was exiled. Her story was told to every child and was a source of inspiration to her. Her grandmother's determination, loyalty, resolve, and sense of purpose through the hard times, the years of hardship she had with her husband were what made him into Genghis Khan. Deep inside, Yasimi wished she could be like her grandmother. She often asked after the secret of what gave her grandmother such a strong spirit. Was it her grandfather Temujin? As a small child, she heard her mother tell her many times that Borte and Temujin shared one soul. Her mother said that every person had half a soul and searched for the other half, but very few find it – those who do become great and change the world. As she grew older, her teachers said that this was just a fantasy and that every person has a whole soul. She often disbelieved her teachers because her grandfather, Temujin, would never have become Genghis Khan if it weren't for her grandmother, Borte. Without Temujin, Borte would have been nothing more than a slave girl to Chiledu, the Merkit Khan.

Am I living with half a soul? Yasimi started to wonder. Perhaps this is the problem, her incomplete soul was seeking its other half. If that was the case, where would she find the other half? Could be it Mahmoud bin Mamdoud, the man whom she was supposed to marry? The only time she met him during the trip from Otrar to Bukhara, she did not get the feeling that he was the one she was looking for, who would complete her as she completed him. When she looked at him, all she saw was an insignificant, shy boy. But even this young man had become unattainable after what happened to her and her companions, though she didn't understand the cause. Even though the commander of the watch told her, after she had been in the prison for several days, that her grandfather had sent spies in the guise of merchants and she had to pay for this hostile action, a cost to be determined by the Sultan.

"I hope he gives you to me, I'd make you my slave girl." The watch captain laughed before continuing the flow of insults. "You? The wife of one of my lord Sultan's grandsons? By God, I didn't think I would live to see the day that a barbarian idol-worshipping Mongol would have an alliance with their Khwarezmian masters through marriage!"

Idol worshippers! Yasimi wanted to tell him that her people did not worship idols, and the merchants they were holding in Bukhara's citadel and those they killed in Otrar were all Muslims just like the Khwarezmians! *If anyone worships idols it is you, and your idol is named "Sultan"!* She wanted to rage at him, but she didn't. She held her silence, she would give them nothing. It was all the same, and the Sultan would decide as he willed. What hope did she have when Tabtinkar's curse followed her everywhere?

The next day, however, she was amazed when the news reached her that the Sultan had made his decision, one that shocked everyone – especially the captain of the watch. "Princess Yasimi shall be released, and she shall be married to Emir Mahmoud bin Mamdoud."

(39)

Dreaming Flow...

The granddaughter of the Mongol Khan was transported from one extreme to the next overnight. It was like waking from a bad dream in which she was a prisoner only to find that she was wife to the grandson of the Sultan of the Khwarezmian Empire. She tried to ask about the merchants who had been thrown in prison, to find out what had happened to them, and if they had also been released. The only answer she got came from the aide to Vizier Najm-Eddin who came to get her from the prison and take her to the harem in Sultan Alaa-Eddin's palace.

"No one is mistreated under Khwarezm's fair justice system."

She tried to get him to explain why this had all happened: why were the merchants accused of being spies? What had they done? The only answer he gave was the same as the first, "No one is mistreated under Khwarezm's fair justice system." It seemed like it was the only thing the man could say.

In the Sultan's palace, Yasimi met a woman in her forties who introduced herself as Darahim, Nouran Khatoun's handmaid. She oversaw all the slave girls and servants in the women's quarters in the palace – the harem. Yasimi had been expecting to meet with her husband Mahmoud, whom she had only seen once, during the caravan trip between Otrar and Bukhara, but Darahim told her that the marriage was a contract only, and her mistress Nouran Khatoun was determined that the marriage would not be consummated until she was certain Yasimi was prepared to be a "good" wife for her grandson. That was why she was in the harem now rather than the Emir's house, which stood next to the Sultan's palace. Here, she would receive a suitable education under her mistress' supervision.

***

Yasimi did not meet Nouran Khatoun until morning rounds the next day, once Darahim had dressed her appropriate to her station as an Emira of Khwarezm rather than a horse herder from the Mongol steppes. The sultan's wife made no effort to hide her disappointment in her grandson's wife, who she did not feel deserved him. To Nouran, that girl was not even good enough to be a simple slave, much less the wife of her beloved grandson whom she had raised on learning, devotion, and piety so he might become a master scholar some day like her father, Qadi Mohamed bin Bushtaq Al-Nishapuri. How could the wife of such a man be an ignorant girl, raised among a people who resembled nothing more than the bygone Bedouins, who had no skills to offer other than the ability to ride a horse like a man? Even so, this is what her husband the sultan had forced her into, encouraged by his mother. *That scorpion of a woman!*

Every time Turkan came to Nouran's mind, she remembered how she had suffered at her hand throughout the years since she married Turkan's son. Turkan was determinedly hostile to her from the first day she came to the palace, and now she wanted to corrupt the life of Mahmoud just because he was her descendant!

"My lady, how are my companions?" Yasimi began her first meeting with Nouran Khatoun in the women's quarter with this question. Darahim, who had been reluctant about the meeting, looked at Yasimi wide-eyed and whispered to her that she must first greet her mother-in-law and kiss her right hand, as she had been taught the day before.

"Let her be, Darahim. The girl wants to be sure her people are well; this is good." Nouran gestured for Yasimi to sit close by, then she went on. "Do not worry, little one; the Lord shall care for them."

"But it was the Sultan who ordered their imprisonment, not the Lord."

"Yasimi!" Darahim hissed, telling the girl that she must show respect to her mistress and master, while the serving girls working in the chamber were shocked by how forward their young mistress was; they couldn't help but smile until they were stopped by their mistress' handmaiden.

Nouran paid little heed to what Yasimi said, she hadn't expected the girl to be very discriminating in her speech. How could an ignorant girl like her control what she says? It was enough that she could speak a language other than her native Mongolian. The moment did impress upon her the need to educate the girl quickly; teaching her the skills required to be a proper wife to her grandson could take years.

"Darahim, did you ask the librarian to send a teacher to begin teaching Princess Yasimi to read and write?"

"And who says I need to learn reading and writing?" Yasimi interjected before Darahim could answer her mistress' question.

"Little one, in our land, for an emira to be unable to read and write would bring shame. I know it might seem tedious to you, but I promise that I will bring you the best teacher, so that you can at least read Allah's book."

"I can already read and write."

"I'm not talking about your mother tongue."

"Neither am I speaking only of Mongol."

Nouran was shocked to hear this. "You can read Arabic script?"

"Arabic as well as Latin and Greek. And Sanskrit, too. I have read the Qur'an, the Torah, and the Gospels as well as the Talmud, the Sutras and the Avesta. I love reading no less than I love riding horses. May I go to the library to see what manuscripts you have? I have heard the library of Bukhara has no equal in the world apart from the library at Baghdad."

Nouran never expected to hear such a thing from Yasimi. How could this girl, born in a land filled with barbarians with no regard for civilization, possess such an education? If she believed what the girl said, then she knew languages that neither Nouran nor Mahmoud had any experience with! *How? It makes no sense!*

"Can you read this book?" Nouran asked, offering the book beside her to Yasimi. She wanted to see for herself if the girl was lying in order to get out of the lessons that were being prepared for her.

"This is the Musnid of Ahmed bin Hanbal. I read a copy of it in Karakorum that a Muslim traveler brought with him when he came from Nishapur."

This princess was a complete surprise to Nouran Khatoun. The only thing she could do was tell her handmaid to cancel the order for a reading and writing teacher. It was clear now that the girl was far beyond that level!

***

Nouran Khatoun and Yasimi grew close over the next few days, particularly when it became clear to Nouran that the girl was unaccountably well educated. She had been taught by several different instructors in her homeland. Not only that, but the girl's skill in some of the subjects the Sultan's wife looked down on, like scholastic theology and chemistry, outstripped both her handmaid and her grandson Mahmoud. But there was one issue that stuck in her throat – the girl's religion. Yasimi told Nouran that she used to believe in Manichaeism, the dualist faith, and that after a passing conversation with Abdel-Rahman, she didn't believe in any religion – and was more confused about the issue than ever. As far as the wife of Sultan Alaa-Eddin Mohamed Khwarezmshah, defender of Islam and all Muslims, daughter to the great scholar, the Qadi Abu Abdallah Mohamed bin Bushtaq Al-Nishapuri, this was unacceptable! The wife of her grandson must be Muslim. That's why she brought the matter up once as they walked through the palace gardens. It was a clear day and the breeze brought with it the scent of jasmine growing on the wooden trellises to provide shade.

"A young lady like you, gifted by God with knowledge and beauty" Nouran began, as she touched Yasimi's luxuriant black hair, "lacks nothing but to follow the true religion."

"If I knew what it was, I would follow it." She answered apologetically.

"It is Islam, little one. How has your sharp mind not brought you to it?"

"My lady Nouran Khatoun, would you permit me a question?"

"My dear, ask what you wish to know."

Yasimi stopped walking and looked into the eyes of her husband's grandmother, the husband she still had not seen since she came to the palace, before asking, "How did your discernment lead you to Islam?"

The question caught the Sultan's wife off-guard. Even so, she had a ready response. "It is one of the blessings Allah has given me, I was raised by Muslim parents."

"What if your parents had followed a faith other than Islam?"

This question seemed strange to Nouran, pointless and unrelated. "I don't understand what you mean. A righteous Muslim will always thank his Lord that he grew up in the shade of the true religion, Islam."

Yasimi paused a moment, considering how to continue. "I've asked several people this same question, each a follower of a different faith. The answer from every one of them was nearly identical to yours. They each believe that their own god has blessed them in particular, out of all the people in the world who believe in other religions, with the one true faith. That is why I always ask – who among them is right? They cannot all be right! If it is a matter of upbringing, then what sin has a person born to misguided parents committed?"

This line of questioning made Nouran uneasy. "This kind of thinking will lead a person astray. The Qur'an says quite clearly that Islam is, without doubt, Allah's religion."

"My lady… the Qur'an provides Muslims with justification because they believe in it. But I…" Yasimi took a deep breath before she went on, as though she wanted to emphasize what she was saying, "am not a Muslim."

With that declaration, Nouran saw that something she thought was going to be a simple matter would not by anything of the sort. Despite all the beautiful things about this girl, she was a danger to her grandson, the boy she had so carefully raised. This kind of talk was frivolous and only served to call one's religion into question! At that moment, filled with worry, Nouran had no choice but to curse her nemesis and the source of her misery:

"God damn you, Turkan, you viper! You have caused this!"

***

After their meeting in the harem garden, the relationship between the Khan's granddaughter and the Sultan's wife began to cool once again. They met less frequently, and only for a few minutes at a time just so Nouran Khatoun could check on Yasimi and make sure she didn't need anything. In fact, there were a great many things the girl wanted to ask about: her husband, whom she had not yet seen, even just to talk to him and get to know him better! The answer was always that they were still too young, and it would be better for them to wait, even if they were technically married. This strange pretext Nouran gave her as an excuse was unconvincing. If he was too young for marriage, then why did they marry her to him? Though he was younger than she, the one time she saw him he seemed older; he was tall and strong. Moreover, he was no younger than her grandfather Temujin had been when he married her grandmother; even her father had married at twelve years old. Her brother was married, too, and he was younger than Mahmoud. Yasimi felt the sting of the excuse given by the Sultan's wife, and she could see that the issue was deeper than a simple matter of her youth. If it weren't, why wouldn't she at least let Yasimi talk to him?

Weeks passed. Every day the Mongol girl felt more like a bird trapped in a golden cage. She wasn't allowed to ride her horse out to the plains as she had done every morning at home; they told her this sort of thing was something only men did. They didn't let her visit the Bukhara library, either, to keep her from associating with the public, particularly now that she had become an emira of the royal family of Khwarezmshah.

One night in the dismal harem, Yasimi didn't feel like sleeping so she wandered the corridors alone. She was pondering the situation she found herself in, so different from what she had expected. The grand palace where she lived was empty, despite being full of people. It was poor, despite its opulence, and dark, despite the bright sunlight streaming in through its ostentatious windows during the day and the opulent chandeliers hanging from the ceilings at night. More than anything just then, she wanted to go back to her tent in Karakorum, but the caravan had left that place and would never return.

As she walked, Yasimi heard a low voice coming from somewhere. The voice was melodious, and the words sounded like it was reciting poetry. She followed the sound, and when she got to the source, she found a serving girl she had never met before. She was a few years older than Yasimi, and was gazing out the window at the full moon as she recited:

You who would ask, what would you know?
Do you walk in this world, or while dreaming flow
Through wakeful nights, eyes unresting,
To find unreachable the object of your questing
When knows the heart, yet still confused
The mind seeks on, yet truth eludes

Goosebumps pricked Yasimi's skin when she heard the poem. She felt like the girl was reciting it for her alone, not to the shining moon in the sky over Bukhara.

"My lady…" the serving girl said when she noticed Yasimi there.

"I'm sorry. I didn't mean to eavesdrop."

"My lady, you don't have to apologize. If anyone should apologize, I should apologize for bothering my lady."

Yasimi approached the serving girl who stayed silent next to the window. The reflected moonlight shining on the girl's pale skin seemed to draw her in.

"You weren't bothering me at all, quite the opposite, in fact. What is your name?"

"Halaja." She answered in a small, anxious voice.

"The verses you were reciting, did you compose them?"

"No, my lady. I wish I could write poetry, but I was only reciting it. Umm Alwafaa wrote it."

"Umm Alwafaa? I haven't heard of her before. Who is she?"

"She is a righteous woman who understands God."

"I'm sorry, but I don't know what you mean when you say she 'understands God'."

"Many people, my lady, learn about God, but there are few who understand him."

"Is there a difference between knowledge and understanding?" Yasimi asked, taken aback.

"Of course there is…" the girl picked up a tray next to her that was covered with cloth before she went on. "My lady, do you know what faluzaj is?"

"I've never heard of it before."

She pulled the cloth off the tray and said, "It's a sort of sweet made from flour, ghee, and honey."

Yasimi looked at what was on the tray she held, then nodded, indicating she knew what faluzaj was.

"Here, my lady, taste it."

Without hesitation, Yasimi reached out to the tray and took a piece to taste. It was delicious, she'd never tasted anything like it before.

"Can you tell the difference, my lady? A moment ago, you didn't know what faluzaj was. Then I told you about it, and you knew. But when you saw it and tasted how good it is, you understood. That is the difference between knowing a thing and understanding it."

"But is it possible for a person to see and taste God?"

"If a person were to use all their senses, my lady, to understand the universe, such a one would understand the God of that universe."

Yasimi was amazed by this serving girl's eloquence. How had they not met before? "Halaja, where did you learn all this?" she asked.

"From Umm Alwafaa, my lady, in Ghazni, before I was captured, after the Khwarezmains had their victory over the Ghorids."

"Was Umm Alwafaa taken as well?"

"God's devotees, my lady. Nothing, no matter how brutishly powerful, can harm them. They are protected by His light. Umm Alwafaa left Ghazni after it fell to the Khwarezmians, though they tried to take her. When they failed, they killed her two disciples on the pretext of heresy. She was very sad and decided to hide in a village called Al-Rabiyya between Bukhara and Ghazni, so no one else would be harmed because of her."

"Why do the Khwarezmians want to harm her?"

Halaja approached Yasimi and cupped her face with the palm of her right hand, "That's a long story, my lady. Why don't you go back to bed for now. Hopefully I will see you again, and I'll tell you about what happened to Umm Alwafaa."

Despite her desire to hear more of Halaja's story, Yasimi could feel her eyelids drooping and suddenly felt very tired. "Alright. Goodnight, then. I'm glad I met you."

With that, she went back to her room and lay down on her bed, surrendering to the deep sleep her exhausted mind needed so badly.

***

Early the next morning, Yasimi woke easily despite only having a few hours of sleep. She felt more rested than usual; she hadn't felt this good since she came to the palace. Maybe the meeting the night before with Halaja had rekindled her curiosity, it had certainly whetted her appetite to know more about Umm Alwafaa. Yasimi wanted to find out more about the woman whose poem had touched her, as though it had been written just for her, giving expression to the root of her concerns.

"Jawahir, could you have Halaja come to me?" she asked her serving girl when she brought breakfast. Yasimi had only eaten a small piece of cheese and some milk mixed with honey. Her appetite to continue the discussion with the eloquent serving girl was greater than her appetite for food.

"Halaja? I'm sorry, my lady, but I don't know any servant in the palace by that name."

Her maid's answer came as a surprise, and she wondered if she had not mispronounced the name. "She is a girl from Ghozni, no older than twenty. Dark skin, thick black hair down to her waist?"

Jawahir thought for a moment, considering the description her lady had given her, but again said she did not know this servant.

"But I met her last night, here in the harem!"

The maid was very embarrassed and did not know how she should respond to her mistress' insistence, but she was relieved to see the Sultan's wife's handmaid enter. "My lady Darahim knows every servant in the palace. Maybe she can help you more than I can."

"What's this, Jawahir? Is there something your mistress needs?" Darahim asked, looking closely at the small maid who was backing away to make room for her near Yasimi. Turning to the Mongol girl, she asked, "Did this idiot servant do something wrong?"

"No, not at all. I was just asking her about a servant girl I met yesterday. I wanted to talk to her again."

"What is her name?"

"I think it was Halaja."

When Yasimi said her name, Darahim was struck dumb and nearly collapsed. If there hadn't been a table nearby to catch herself on…

"Leave now, Jawahir. I will see to your mistress."

Darahim followed her and closed the door when she left, then approached Yasimi. "Will you please describe the serving girl you met yesterday for me?"

"She was a young girl with dark skin, a few years older than me, with long black hair."

"Impossible!" Darahim cried, cutting her off unintentionally. She quickly apologized for her rudeness.

"What makes it impossible?" Yasimi asked urgently, surprised by the handmaiden's reaction.

"My lady… What you just said, it's… it cannot be. The serving girl you described, she's…" Darahim paused before she finished very reluctantly, "She is no longer alive!"

***

Yasimi couldn't decide which was the more surprising, that she had seen a girl who died some years before, or the reason why that poor girl had died. Together they formed a quandary she couldn't understand. She was only a little over fourteen years old, but she had seen death caused by many things, some stranger than others. One thing was constant about death, though – no one came back. So how had that girl, whose beheading had been ordered by the Sultan, have returned? Yasimi had seen her plainly, just as she saw Darahim now. How was this possible? Every detail Yasimi recalled was perfectly clear. Her black hair, her dark skin, where she came from. Even her relationship with the woman, Umm Alwafaa. Everything was exactly right, as though she knew the dead girl. When Halaja had spoken of what Umm Alwafaa had taught her, Sultan Alaa-Eddin Mohamed Khwarezmshah ordered her execution by beheading because of the "Sufi heresy" she was spreading in his palace; how could the "Protector of the Faith" allow such blasphemy in his own home?

(40)
Questions without Answers

He seemed to want to be arrested and thrown in prison. Or maybe he didn't have the power to pull off another magical feat as he had done before. Whichever it was, something had changed since his encounter with that strange apparition outside the citadel, or so it seemed to Murad as he considered Abdel-Rahman's current situation. He was in a dark cell in the citadel. He was silent and still, only getting up to pray before going right back to his posture, sitting on his knees like he would when reciting the *tashahhud*, the testimony of faith, before bowing prostrate during prayer. *What's wrong with you?* Murad tried to ask several times, but he only ever got one answer: "The cycle is not yet complete."

What cycle was he talking about? From Murad's point of view, things were getting worse and more confusing. Every time he felt like he took a step in the right direction, he found himself being pulled back several more steps. When he felt like he was coming close to answering a question, a dozen new ones cropped up, like this whole thing would never end. Murad was aware of the fact that Abdel-Rahman knew far more than he let on, but there had been one thing that seemed to puzzle the strange man – or at least to have caught him off-guard: what happened outside the citadel, especially when he told him that he thought Yasimi might have seen him.

Something had forced Abdel-Rahman to reevaluate his plans, Murad thought, but what? Whatever it was, could it have been what made him wait for the soldiers to come to the inn so they could arrest him? If there was one thing Murad had learned from being in that man's company, it was that he never did anything arbitrarily. Every move he made was calculated, like he was executing a carefully designed overarching plan that accounted for every detail. Had he planned to come back to Bukhara, to be thrown in prison, after helping the Mongol caravan's merchant sheikh escape? Or had some emergency come up, making him restructure things? Questions, questions, questions! The more questions there were, the fewer the answers! If he has a physical head, Murad felt like it would have exploded from confusion and frustration. His confusion came from everything happening to him and around him in this strange situation he found himself in. His frustration stemmed from his inability to do anything but watch. It was like he was being forced to watch a play from beginning to end, shackled to his seat, not allowed to move without permission. And he didn't know how the play had begun, or what it was about.

***

As the days became weeks, and the weeks months, Murad watched Abdel-Rahman and Mohamed Attousi – who was also quiet and contemplative – showing signs of wasting away because of the meager rations. *The way this lad has accepted what has happened to him since he was so recently released from prison is amazing!* Murad thought that after he spent nearly a year in prison following what happened to his teacher, the qadi Wasil bin Ghilan, and after the emotional suffering during that terrible time, the youth would never have willingly gone back to the same place. He was sure that when Abdel-Rahman gave Mohamed permission to leave on his own – and gave him the means to do so – he would have left all this misery far behind. But he didn't. He chose to stay. *Is he stupid or is there something more to it? What would make a young man like him accept this kind of hardship?* Murad tried to fathom it, but he just couldn't. *Mohamed Attousi must be an odd duck, after all – birds of a feather flock together!* Everything here is strange. The time, the place, and the people; and as if all of that wasn't bizarre enough, that strange entity showed itself to him when he tried to help Yasimi. It tried to seduce him, and when that didn't work, it tried to kill him! It looked something like a shadow cast by an invisible person, and it was dark and terrifying. *What could it be?* Turning what little he knew over in his mind, he remembered what Abdel-Rahman had said when he asked if it was a djinn. *It is a much more dangerous entity.* What in creation was more dangerous than a djinn that Murad had never heard of? Questions,

questions, and more questions! And every single question sparked another after it.

While he reviewed recent events, Murad noticed something else. While that entity was talking to him about what happened in Otrar, his vision shifted there – as though he had traveled through time, or time had moved around them. He saw something that had happened in the past as though it were happening in the present. Was he seeing things through the entity's point of view? Maybe it had been a witness to what happened. This gave Murad an idea, *Can I do the same thing? Can I see things that I've seen before as though they were happening again as I watch?* If he could do that, maybe he could find something he missed in the course of events; maybe he could shed some light on the riddle he found himself in the middle of. Maybe he could even see things from a different point of view, like someone watching a video recording; it might reveal something he hadn't seen the first time while things were still unfolding. Murad hoped he might be able to examine the events during his last few days in Riyadh in minute detail. *If I could go back to the past and see things knowing what I know now, I might interpret them differently.* The instant the idea occurred to him, strangely, Abdel-Rahman and Mohamed Attousi vanished! The entire world around him had changed. At first, he thought maybe it would take him back to Riyadh, that he would wake up at last to find that this really was just a dream, that there was no Abdel-Rahman, no strange entity, nor even Yasimi. But when he looked around himself after his vision cleared, he was not in Riyadh nor in any place he recognized, though he knew some of the people he could see in this forgotten moment from his life quite well.

(41)
The Future's Past

The guest finished eating. Before he left the hall, he said, "Allah has been generous with you. I've never had such delicious manti shish barak before. Thank you."

"You haven't eaten anything, Tarek." The house's owner said, then looked at the guest's son, "you haven't eaten either. You must both have eaten at the hotel."

What he was looking at was a humble house. Two men and a boy of about twelve years. Murad recognized the boy immediately; it was him when he was younger. The man with him was his father, Tarek. But where was this? Murad didn't remember it at all, it was like it had been wiped from his memory. Then something came to him that he hadn't thought about much before. This wasn't just something that he didn't remember from his life, he couldn't remember much from his life at all! Just a flash here and there. He was seeing these things now as though they were happening for the first time, despite how familiar they felt. He knew that what he saw now *had* happened to him, though he remembered nothing about it.

"You haven't said. Did you enjoy Bukhara?" the owner of the house asked the boy who smiled shyly before answering yes.

"Really, Abdel-Jalil, Murad and I have enjoyed our time with you. We wouldn't want to keep you from your work."

"Say nothing of it, man. We're family. You don't know how happy the family was when I told them that I was finally able to reach our great-grandfather's descendants who had emigrated to Mecca a hundred years ago!"

"Allah be praised, if the Soviet Union hadn't collapsed, and Uzbekistan gained its independence, you wouldn't have come for the Hajj and reached out to me. I never would have brought Murad to Bukhara to connect with the rest of the family."

Why couldn't he remember anything about this trip with his father to Bukhara? Why, when he wanted to see recent events in Riyadh, had he ended up here? Murad didn't understand what was happening. He thought he might have been able to control which memories he saw, but here he was watching something he didn't even remember. He didn't even know how he got here – but something important occurred to him just then: did this mean he wouldn't be able to get back to ancient Bukhara? Back to Abdel-Rahman and Yasimi?

"We have to get going early tomorrow. It is a long trip, and the roads aren't very good. It will take ten hours or so." Abdel-Jalil told his relatives from Saudi Arabia.

"I thought it was here in Bukahra, or somewhere nearby."

"No, it is the far eastern part of Uzbekistan, near the border with Kazakhstan."

"Father, what's so important about this shrine?" Murad asked timidly.

"It is the shrine of our ancestor, Qutuz, the progenitor of our family. It has been there for centuries." He told his son, then directed his attention back to the owner of the house, "But what are the secrets of the place where the shrine is located? Is there some historic significance?"

"I really don't know. The shrine is in a remote village where some members of our family used to live before they left during the Soviet era. That's all my father remembered. I'm not even certain we'll find it still standing. We will be the first three members of the family to visit this place in generations."

***

The geography was just the same: deserts surrounded by barren mountains and interspersed by huge oases shifting to flat steppe land. Just what Murad had seen when he was traveling with the two caravans, Jalal-Eddin's and the Mongol merchants, from Otrar to Bukhara, but this time they were driving in an old Russian-made car instead of in a camel caravan. There were more towns, too, along the road to eastern Uzbekistan.

After a nearly ten-hour drive, the car stopped next to an old stone building on an abandoned corner of a farm village near a railroad line.

"They say that in the ancient past the Silk Road came through here. We're also not far from the ancient city of Otrar; its ruins are in Kazakhstan just over the border."

After hearing what Abdel-Jalil said, Murad had a shocking thought. If he imagined there was no town here, and removed all signs of the twentieth century... this was exactly where he had found himself after he was dropped off the Ghanim Elsaaidi tower!

Tarek Qutuz approached the shrine, placing his right arm around his son Murad's shoulders, then he started reading the poem inscribed on the walls aloud.

"You who would ask, what would you know?
Do you walk in this world, or while dreaming flow
Through wakeful nights, eyes unresting
To find unreachable the object of your questing
When knows the heart, yet still confused
The mind seeks on, yet truth eludes"

Tarek looked at Abdel-Jalil and asked, "Do you know anything about this poem?"

The man shook his head no. "The shrine, as you see, has been abandoned for years. If you hadn't asked my father about it when we came for the pilgrimage, I probably would never have heard of it." Abdel-Jalil smiled and went on. "It looks like the branch of the family that went to Mecca is more concerned about our past than the branch that stayed in Bukhara."

Murad didn't remember any of what he was seeing, it seemed like watching a movie for the first time. Did it really happen? Was it wiped from his memory? Or was everything he saw just fantasy, and it never really

270

happened? He searched his memory looking for an answer to the new questions pounding through his mind, but... nothing. Nothing at all. Why couldn't he remember anything from his childhood? Where had the memories gone?

As he weathered this new storm of questions, the sky overhead went dark and he found himself leaving the men, the boy, the shrine, and the world that had been surrounding him. He returned to the dark prison to find himself standing with Abdel-Rahman and Mohamed Attousi. They were standing next to an open door, no guards in sight – there were no soldiers in the entire dungeon!

(42)
A Message to be Sent

Never had Sultan Alaa-Eddin Mohamed felt as angry as he did when the envoy of Genghis Khan came with a message demanding he hand over the governor of Otrar, Yanal Khan, to face justice for falsely accusing the Mongol merchants of being spies and executing some of them though they had done nothing wrong. *After honoring the Khan's granddaughter by marrying her to my grandson, this toad comes, demanding retribution for a handful of merchants who weren't even part of his clan, who didn't even share his religion? Is he insane?! Doesn't he know I can make him crawl if I wished? Make him eat my shoes? Make him an example for others?* The Sultan looked at the Mongol ambassador who was standing there in his wretched clothes and his uncouth appearance, then came up with the appropriate response to the letter from the Mongol Khan – a response that only a savage like him who dares defy their Khwarezmian masters would understand!

"Swordsman!" the Sultan cried, then turned to Vizier Najm-Eddin. "Let my response to the letter from this idiot Khan be the head of his messenger! Maybe then he will learn how to speak to his betters."

(43)
The Tides of War

Yanal Khan heard the Mongol army was coming with Geghis Khan himself at the head, but he did not want to wait until they reached the walls of Otrar. Instead, he sent his army out to meet them. The Mongols may have been able to conquer the Tatar and Merkit tribes on the steppes, but they would not be able to stand up to an army led by warriors from the Kanakali tribe. *Oh, how they will suffer!* This was a great opportunity for the governor of Otrar. He would defeat the Mongols and extend his territory to the east where no Khwarezmian or Muslim army had been able to overcome before. If he could decisively defeat the Mongols here, nothing would be able to stand up to him until he got to China – and that was the greater prize! Then he would finally be able to achieve his forefathers' dreams of establishing a great Kanakali empire, once the new territories took their independence from the Khwarezmians. It was a great dream, and the only thing keeping him from making it reality was an army of horse breeders from the steppes, tent-dwellers led by a "Mongol toad!"

***

The commander of Otrar's army, Othman bin Tarkhan, looked out over the Mongol horsemen facing off against his soldiers, swords bare. There were a lot of them, but not as many as his army – more than forty thousand cavalry and infantry. He did a simple calculation and estimated they had about ten thousand mounted men. A quarter of those would fall to arrows before they reached his lines, the rest would fare no better. The commander laughed at the Mongols who were so good at raids yet understood nothing of the art of war and battle. *They think courage is enough to win a battle. They don't know it is much more complex than that!*

The commander ordered his archers to loose their arrows. As he had calculated, about a quarter of the Mongol horsemen fell. Then a group of spearmen advanced. *Another quarter will fall, leaving half of their original strength. What idiots! It looks like this battle will be over quickly.* All Othman bin Tarkhan could do was laugh at the naiveté of the army and the commander who came against him; he had thought the Mongols more skilled than what he saw now!

The two armies met. Blood flowed on both sides. The Mongol horsemen carried no shields, wore no chain mail, just hardened leather. The men of the Otrar army seemed better equipped and more professional.

His second in command, wanting a quick end to the imbalanced battle, asked, "My lord commander, shall we put an end to them now? They've lost many of their mounted men, they will not be able to stand up to our cavalry."

"Alright." The commander said, "send the signal." He was growing suspicious of what he saw. It seemed far easier than he had been anticipating. *How did the armies of China and Karakhatta, both more skilled than these men, fall before them?*

The Kanakali cavalry swept through the remaining Mongol horsemen, quickly routing them and sending them running back to their bases, pursued hotly by the Otrar army. Their shouts could be heard now, gleeful at the quick victory, though the commander's concern grew at the site of this rout which came far faster than he had expected.

As they pursued the Mongols, the Kanakali cavalry rode with swords bare, ready to take their enemies' heads, as was the standing order. They hadn't ridden far, though, before their horses began to slow, burdened by the weight of their riders; something that didn't seem to be affecting the Mongols. Soon enough, though, the Kanakali saw the Mongols beginning to slow, then came something unexpected.

Shouts of "It's a trap! Trap!" came from many voices as arrows plowed into the Kanakali cavalry from behind. Clusters of Mongol horsemen had come out from their hiding places behind the hills. The Mongols were now behind and in front of them, and they were all firing their bows from horseback as they rode, controlling the horses with their legs only.

As the arrows pierced their bodies, the cavalrymen began to fall one after another like leaves from a tree in Autumn. As the Otrar commanding general had anticipated, the battle did not last long. But it was his own army that was annihilated.

***

Yanal Khan was unable to believe what he saw as he watched from a window in his palace that overlooked the city wall. The Mongol army surrounded Otrar as far as the eye could see in every direction. Their numbers were impossible to count. *Where did Genghis Khan get so many men?*

It wasn't just soldiers and horsemen, either. They had every kind of siege equipment: trebuchets, battering rams, ballistae, siege towers and other things he had never seen before. At any rate, what he saw was not a handful of plainsmen raiding the great city; it was an inexorable, unparalleled professional army. Even so, Yanal Khan's only choice was to resist. He knew that the Mongol general, Jochi, Genghis Khan's oldest son, always gave the people of the city two choices: absolute surrender, delivering Yanal Khan to the general to pay for what he did to the Mongol merchants, or the complete destruction of the city and all its residents. Either way, the governor would lose. He had to fight back. Maybe he could buy time for his nephew, Sultan Alaa-Eddin, to send aid.

The siege went on day after day. The city and its walls enduring bombardment from stones and heavy bolts from the ballistae along with barrels filled with a black substance unknown to the people that caused an explosion if it came in contact with fire, burning everyone in the vicinity. The terrifying sound of the explosions jarred soldier and citizen alike. Morale sank lower with each passing day that no relief came from Bukhara, Samarkand, or any other city in the Empire. The people were taken by despair and they started to speak of surrender, something the governor did not take well. He strongly refused to give in, and he ordered the beheading of anyone heard uttering that treasonous word. Even so, what Yanal Khan feared eventually came to pass. After a month of siege and constant bombardment, Otrar's defenses were overcome, and the Mongols entered the city. From his balcony, the governor saw troops swarm over the city like locusts leaving destruction in their wake. Wave after wave of horsemen swept in, destroying and burning buildings, killing anyone they found. The Mongols' promise was being fulfilled before his eyes.

Yanal Khan didn't know what to do. He was terrified by what he saw, frozen in place by fear. It was like his feet were nailed to the floor. Several horsemen entered the palace unhindered; the guards had fled. The governor started looking all around, looking for a way out. The sound of pounding feet reached his ears as they approached the room where he was. He didn't know what to do! Moments passed, and two Mongol warriors came in brandishing their swords. What should he do? He kept looking around. What could he do? His heart was about to beat its way out of his chest, and he still didn't know what to do. Looking behind himself, he gathered his remaining strength to force his legs to move and turned to run to the balcony. Glancing back, he saw the two warriors calmly walking in his direction, then he looked from the high balcony to the ground far below. It was a very long way, more than four stories. He looked back at the Mongols again, then made up his mind. He knew that anything – anything – would be better than to be captured by those barbarians.

(44)
100,000 Horsemen

The tragedy of Otrar's army came as a shock to Sultan Alaa-Eddin Mohamed. He would never have imagined that the best Kanakali cavalrymen could be destroyed by those "uncivilized" Mongols. News quickly followed of the siege of Otrar, followed by the city's collapse at the hands of Jochi, Yasimi's father. Then came news of his uncle Yanal Khan's death and the complete destruction of the city. For a moment he wished he had just left the Mongol girl to rot in the Bukhara's citadel. As if the news they brought him weren't enough, word also reached him that plagued his rest: a vast army, led by Genghis Khan and larger than the one that brought down Otrar – estimated to be nearly 100,000 strong and most on horseback, was a few days away from Bukhara. "Where did the Mongols come up with so many men?! How did they travel so far so fast?" Alaa-Eddin nearly went mad, he never dreamed things would come to this. *Impossible! How could the Mongols penetrate his territory like this? How?*

"My lord, the army is camped between Bukhara and Samarkand. I think it would be best to gather under a single banner in the impenetrable fortress at Samarkand." This advice came to him from General

Sanjar, but the Sultan was unconvinced; doing so would mean leaving Bukhara unprotected, ripe for the taking.

"By Allah, I will not! It will not be said that I gave Bukhara to the Mongols!" the Sultan stated emphatically, refusing the suggestion of his army's commander.

"My lord, if the city falls, it would be better than allowing the entire empire to fall. Divided, our armies will not be able to stand before the Mongol army. They will wipe them out, one after the other. We must join forces, my lord."

"I told you no! The walls around our cities are great. We have supplies to survive a prolonged siege. We will leave Bukhara's army in place to protect the city and destroy the Mongol army." The Sultan declared, refusing any talk of withdrawing the army.

"Then, my lord, at least you should go to Samarkand, to assemble an army there from the rest of the Empire. Then you could take on the Mongols and break the siege of Bukhara if it goes on too long."

Sultan Alaa-Eddin Mohamed fell silent for a moment, considering what he knew of the situation. Not long ago, it was he who raided the surrounding nations. Everyone feared him, including the Abbasid Caliph. Now, he was being forced to flee like a sheep before wolves. *How did it come to this? How?*

***

Nouran Khatoun refused to flee to Samarkand with her husband, his mother, and the rest of his wives. She was determined to stay in Bukhara. She would not leave the people of the city to face the Mongol threat alone. This is what she said when Alaa-Eddin Mohamed told her of the retreat. Though he refused to allow her to stay at first, his mother quickly convinced him that it might be for the best to have some of the royal family to stay in Bukhara, to stiffen the resolve of the defenders. With Nouran's popularity among the city's residents, she was the right person to stay – and she wasn't alone in refusing to run. Her grandson, Mahmoud bin Mamdoud was set on staying with her, which only served to increase Turkan Khatoun's pleasure. The farther the Sultan was from Nouran and her offspring, the better as far as she – and the crown prince, her favorite grandson, Ghiyath-Eddin – where concerned.

One last thing remained for the Sultan's wife to handle with great resolve... the fate of Yasimi. When Alaa-Eddin Mohamed wanted, with his mother's urging, to punish the daughter of Jochi, commander of the army that killed his uncle in Otrar, she absolutely refused. She stood between him and the girl to protect her, reciting the words of Allah almighty: No soul bears the sin of another soul. She was well aware that this kind of argument would not stand in the way of Turkan's revenge for the murder of her brother. She ordered her servant Lu'lu to hide Yasimi somewhere no one could reach her, far from the palace, until her mother-in-law left the city. Fortunately for the girl, Turkan Khatoun and her son the Sultan did not stay long in Bukhara – the massive Mongol hordes were almost there.

(45)
Fallen City

Something was going on outside. Mohamed Attousi could hear the soldiers' shouts and he could hear them moving around, both sounding more and more stressed as the days passed. It sounded like something serious was coming. The young man tried to ask the guard who brought him food and water, but it was no use. The guard quickly dashed back up, not wanting to stay in the darkness of the citadel's dungeon any longer than he had to. The place seemed empty now that the three or four guards who had always been on duty were missing. Days passed in this way until the day finally came when no guard appeared whatsoever. It seemed they had forgotten all about the occupants of the dark cells. Tension started to creep into the minds of the prisoners, who began shouting for the guards who had forgotten them, asking for water and food. The next evening, after Mohamed decided that they were doomed without water and food, Abdel-Rahman stood from where he had been kneeling and went to the cell door. He opened it effortlessly, or so it appeared, and the young man with him was completely stunned.

"How...? Did the guard forget to lock the door?"

Abdel-Rahman didn't answer him, but he waited for a few moments beside the open door, as though he was expecting something. Then he simply walked out into the hall and headed for the stairs leading up to the next floor and the main door of the prison.

***

What they saw in the front hall was ghastly. Mohamed Attousi had never seen so many corpses in one place in his entire life. They were surrounded by streams of blood, severed limbs, and organs spilling from mortal wounds. He spun, unable to believe his eyes, but the sight went on as far as he could see. The grounds outside were littered with hundreds of bodies, all citadel soldiers and guards.

"What happened here?" Mohamed asked the only other living person on the citadel's grounds, though he knew Abdel-Rahman had been with him inside the prison when this tragedy struck.

"If you don't want to end up like them, I advise you to hurry away from this place. Otherwise, the people who did this will think you a guard who managed to escape their blades. I'm sure they would be quick to rectify such an oversight."

As soon as he finished speaking, Abdel-Rahman walked quickly away with Mohamed following in his wake, leaving the citadel's grounds.

"Merciful Allah!" The young man's heart dropped when they left the citadel and saw the corpses of children, women, and men; all the people of Bukhara, innumerable bodies heaped in the streets around him as far as the eye could see. At first, Mohamed wasn't sure he could continue walking, that his legs wouldn't be able to bear his weight. The sight he beheld all around him was beyond horrifying. He even considered the idea that Judgment Day had come! If atrocity could be made manifest, it could be no worse than the vision before him now.

"We have to move now. If not…" Abdel-Rahman took Mohamed's arm to encourage him to move. The young man freed himself from Abdel-Rahman's grip and looked at him, refusing to move; the expression on his face mixed rage and mourning.

"Leave me alone!" Mohamed Attousi shouted, then he turned and walked alone towards even more bodies laying on the edges of the street. He started digging through them, turning some over, looking for signs of life any time he thought he heard a moan. The ones who perpetrated this tragedy were masters of the craft. Not a single person was left alive. Every sword stroke, every spear thrust was precise and accurate, ensuring a swift and inevitable death.

After a few moments of this, Mohamed heard voices coming from a nearby house. For a minute he thought they might be survivors of this unprovoked massacre. The error in his thinking was clear in a moment, however. He saw a man leave the house. He was not dressed like a resident of Bukhara, and he was heavily armed. Another man came out after him, dressed the same and similarly armed. Mohamed froze in place, thinking they might not notice him in the dark of the night. Again, he saw the error in his thinking when they both turned in his direction, drawing their swords.

***

The first Mongol warrior shouted at Mohamed in a language he didn't understand, but the look on the man's face and the gestures he made were clear enough – he was asking "What are you doing here?" or "Who are you?" or something along those lines. Mohamed shook his head trying to indicate that he didn't understand the warrior's language. This only served to agitate him further, prompting him to bring his blade to Mohamed's throat and shout some more. Mohamed didn't know what to do or how he could respond to the man's angry questions. He tried to sneak a glance to the right and left, looking for Abdel-Rahman, though he had not heard or seen any sign of him right before these men appeared. *I hope you haven't left me like I told you to!* For an instant he felt like his time had come and he would become just another corpse with its throat cut among the many all around him. He had just begun the *tashahhud* when he heard Abdel-Rahman's voice behind him, speaking a language he didn't know – but the man holding the sword at his throat and his companion both seemed to understand him. He lowered the sword immediately and backed away looking afraid. Abdel-Rahman kept talking, repeating the phrase over and over in a loud voice, striking greater fear into the two warriors.

"Zay awa'il bee amaf tami! Zay awa'il bee amaf tami!"

Mohamed Attousi didn't understand what he was saying, but the sentence he repeated over and over had a strange effect on the men, it looked like they were ready to collapse in fear. It only took a few moments for them to flee in abject terror.

Mohamed didn't need to ask his question, the expression on his face told the story of his shock eloquently enough.

"Bukhara fell to the Mongols after a short savage siege." Abdel-Rahman answered.

"Mongols? But… where was the Khwarezmian army? How could a city like Bukhara, with its massive walls, fall like this? And to them?"

"I think you know the answer to that question yourself. Bukhara and other cities in the empire fell long ago. They fell when the people willingly bowed to the subjugation of their rulers and religious scholars."

Mohamed fell silent, in a state of shock over what he had seen and heard. Then he looked to Abdel-Rahman and asked, "What will we do now? Shall we stay?"

"No. It is time for us to leave Bukhara. But first, we have one last stop to make at Moussa's Inn."

(46)
Circle without End

Though many things were still unclear to Murad Qutuz, he began to understand one important thing: his presence here was not random or meaningless. There was a strong tie binding him to this place. What he did not yet understand was why he was here at this time. He believed, though he didn't know why, that the key to understanding his current situation was the answer to this quandary: *why now*?

Throughout human history, some things have remained incomprehensible, mysteries that have made people ask questions and do research. The strange thing was that even if Murad's quest led him to an answer to this conundrum, he knew it would just uncover new questions that had no answers. This is how it has been throughout the ages, people ask, they seek, they ask, then seek some more – like going around and around in a never-ending circle. Who am I? Where did I come from? Where am I going? What is the secret of this universe I see around me? Question after question, building up, prodding humanity into motion to discover themselves and the world that gave them life. Murad moved in the same way in order to discover the truth of who he was. That most important of questions, posed by Abdel-

Rahman when they first met in that uninhabited place outside Otrar.

***

"Put up your weapons and go back to where you came from if you want to see tomorrow's sunrise. Otherwise, you will meet a fate worse than theirs. A slow and terrible death! A slow and terrible death!"

For a second, Murad thought he was looking at someone other than Abdel-Rahman, the man he knew and had traveled with through the recent months. He even felt the same fear as the two Mongol warriors as he repeated the same phrase, "A slow and terrible death." With each repetition, the words seemed to create a tremor in the earth that shook the core of the men's being.

It was strange that these two heavily armed Mongol warriors would fear the words of an unarmed man. Murad questioned how that could be. Though he was starting to feel the answer deep inside, after months of accompanying Abdel-Rahman and seeing his nearly incomprehensible powers – though he kept trying to figure them out. He had been saved from that entity by creating some kind of bright flash or concentrated energy that frightened that dark phantasm, or burned it, or whatever it did. It had happened right here, but in broad daylight, without anyone present seeing it. And now, some two months later, what he had just witnessed by dark of night – nothing about it was surprising.

Murad also knew that the timing of Abdel-Rahman's recent escape from prison was not a matter of chance. He went in there for a reason, if only to be there until the time came to finish what he came for. Pieces were falling into place for Murad whenever he seriously thought about Abdel-Rahman's behavior, and so when the latter told Mohamed Attousi they still had one stop to make before leaving Bukhara, he was not surprised. In fact, he had all but anticipated this trip.

(47)
Flight

I f she didn't want them to end up prisoners, Nouran Khatoun knew that her only option was to leave the palace along with her grandson Mahmoud. Once the Mongols broke through the outer wall of the city, the fall of Bukhara was inevitable, it was just a matter of time. Especially when she heard that High Qadi Abu Abdel-Aziz Yahya bin Rihan had struck a deal with the city watch that they would form a delegation to negotiate a surrender with Genghis Khan in order to "get out of this ordeal with minimal losses," or so he said. Trying to resist would be too costly, too costly by far. As for the matter of defensive jihad raised by the commander of the city's army, who refused surrender on principle, Qadi Yahya recited from the Qur'an, saying, "and cast not yourselves to perdition with your own hands," giving himself and the merchants of Bukhara the excuse they needed to surrender, which was what they wanted all along.

When Nouran realized what was going on, she told Mahmoud everything in complete secrecy after sending all her remaining handmaidens and servants away. As for Yasimi, it was a simple matter – or so she thought. The girl would go back to her family, the victorious conquerors, particularly since the marriage to her grandson had never been anything but a pretense; they had never consummated the marriage. What happened, however, was that as Nouran started to leave, Yasimi surprised her. *How did she know? Who told her?* She didn't know what to do when the girl appeared before her just as she was ready to take Mahmoud to Moussa's Inn before fleeing Bukhara for Ghazni, where her son Jalal-Eddin Manguberdi was. The real surprise came when the girl asked to go with them.

"How did you learn about this? I told no one!"

"Were I in your shoes, I would do no different. Ghazni is farthest away from the Mongol army, and your son is the governor there." She went on, sensing Nouran's apprehension. "There is no place for me now among the Mongols. My marriage to Mahmoud made me one of you. My place is with you now."

Everything about this girl is strange! Her people are winning, and she wants to flee with the vanquished? Yasimi was a confusing puzzle for Nouran, one she couldn't comprehend. Despite her suspicions about the girl in the beginning, she believed what Yasimi said when she looked into her wide eyes. Nouran Khatoun was completely convinced that no matter how skilled the tongue could be at deception; the eyes could never lie.

***

Abdel-Rahman left Mohamed Attousi in the stables to get the horses ready, then he went into the attached inn, empty of patrons other than two women and a young man hiding in a room they had rented from the inn's owner. Moussa had decided to stay, despite the wealth he had come into. Yasimi was the first to see Abdel-Rahman when she went to bring food and drink. She was so shocked, she nearly dropped the dishes she carried, but she managed to keep her grip on them at the last moment. She had thought she would never see him again, particularly after hearing news of his arrest. The last thing she expected after that was to meet him at the inn under these trying circumstances.

"What are you doing here?" She blurted without thinking.

"I came to accompany you all to Ghazni."

His answer was another shock, as unanticipated as his sudden appearance. Nouran Khatoun told her that no one knew of their plans. Yasimi didn't know how to respond, especially since she had promised to keep this secret. Her confusion didn't last long, however, as Nouran appeared suddenly along with her grandson, as though she had heard the conversation from her room.

"You are alright!" Nouran's surprise was clear. "But where is Mohamed Attousi? Did he…" she didn't finish the question, afraid of the answer she did not want to hear.

"He is well also. But none of us will remain so for long if we don't get moving right away."

"How did you know? What is your secret?" Mahmoud bin Mamdoud asked. Since he first saw Abdel-Rahman, he had seen inexplicable and extraordinary things happen around him. These two questions were like a cloud that wouldn't dissipate and allow his mind to clear.

"The road to your destination is long. Maybe you'll find the answer you seek as we travel."

This wasn't the answer the boy wanted. For some reason, he suspected that "the destination" that Abdel-Rahman was talking about was not the one he meant when talking to his grandmother.

Conclusion of Chapter One

"Will the wolves win?" Borte asked the Shaman, Tabtinkar, when he left his habitual seclusion, and came to sit on the hill overlooking the steppes to the west of Karakorum.

"Nothing will be that has not already been." He answered without looking at her, contemplating the far horizon as though he watched something happening there that only he could see.

"What is it that will happen, and has already been?"

The Shaman didn't answer, remaining silent. A few minutes earlier, he had been in his usual trance state, traveling between worlds while seated in his tent. His shadow friend had been gone long, but he found the being returning from the other world. It was in bad shape, having nearly vanished among the waves in the sky because of the stranger's actions. What power did that stranger hold? Where did he obtain it? Tabtinkar had seen the sudden light and what it did to his shadow ally; he saw another being manifest a physical body for a moment before returning to its hidden world. In that fraction of an instant he had seen its face before it vanished, the Shaman saw everything. Tabtinkar knew what his friend, this dark, disembodied spirit as he had been calling it, had been hiding from him. He knew at that instant that the two opposites had started out as one. Neither would have existed without the other.

Main Characters

(in order of appearance)

The Modern World

- Morad Qutuz
- Dr. Hadeel – Morad's one-time intended
- Wajih Zakry – Hadeel's brother-in-law
- Hanna Zakry – Wajih's wife, Hadeel's sister
- Nadim Alzoud – Morad's childhood friend
- Sheikh Ghanim Elsaaidi – A fabulously wealthy Sheikh, owner of the hospital where Morad works in Riyadh (among other things)
- Nasser Alquwit – Advisor to Sheikh Ghanim
- Sheikh Ibrahim Assanduq (Abu-Abdallah)
- Sarah Alquwit – Sheikh Ganim's wife
- Virginia Tabt – American polymath genius and prodigy
- Mohamed – Tunisian waiter

The Mongols and the Caravan

- Borte – Tamujin's wife
- Tamujin – Genghis Khan (Genghis means *universe ruler*, and Khan is a Mongol leader)

- Yesugei Khan – Khan of the Merkit tribe, kidnapper of Borte
- Tabtinkar – Mongol Shaman
- Jochi – Son of Borte, paternity in doubt between Yesugei and Tamujin
- Yasimi – Gheghis Khan's granddaughter, Jochi's daughter
- Mohamed bin Ishaq Elbukhari – senior Shiekh of the Mongol merchants

The Khwarezmian Empire

The royal family

- Khwarezmshah – Sultan of Khwarezm, Alaa-Eddin Mohamed
- Yanal Khan – Maternal Uncle of the Sultan, governor of Otrar
- Turkan Khatoun – mother of Sultan Alaa-Eddin (Khatoun is title given to female nobles, equivalent to Khan in men)
- Nouran Khatoun – Second wife of Sultan Alaa-Eddin, Emira (princess / female leader)
- Jalal-Eddin Manguberdi – Son of Sultan Alaa-Eddin and Nouran Khatoun, first son of the Sultan, Emir (Prince)
- Qatr-Elnada – First wife of Sultan Alaa-Eddin
- Ghiyath-Eddin – Son of Qatr-Elnada and Sultan Alaa-Eddin, second son of the Sultan

- Mamdoud bin Mahmoud – Grandson of Nouran Khatoun through her daughter, Fayrouz, and son-in-law Mahmoud

Khwarezmian Court

- High Qadi Abu Abdel-Aziz Yahya bin Rihan / Abu Abdel-Aziz – Senior Qadi (religious scholar/judge) of the Khwarezmian Court
- Vizier Khalid bin Mansour – Advisor to the governor of Otrar
- Vizier Najm-Eddin Kablak – Advisor to the Sultan

Others

- Abdel-Rahman – appears to Morad before joining the Mongols; holds unusual knowledge and abilities
- Qadi Wasil bin Ghilan – widely respected scholar, executed by the Sultan for heresy
- Mohamed Attousi – pupil/disciple of Wasil bin Ghilan

A note about names

In the Arab world, it is very common and demonstrates a personal knowledge of a person to refer to them with a name that indicates their firstborn son. In our story, Sheikh Ibrahim is called *Abu-Abdallah* by Sheikh Ghanim as a way of trying to calm the situation during his dialog with Virginia Tabt; this indicates two things, Sheikh Ibrahim has a son named Abdallah, and Sheikh Ghanim was showing warmth and calling on their personal connection to tone down the rhetoric.

Translators Afterward

I have always loved to read.

In my early childhood, I read dictionaries, encyclopedias, and my mother's dime-store novels. I was ten years old, suffering from ulcers of all things, when my mother brought me the brand-new David Eddings book *Pawn of the Prophecy* to distract me from the discomfort. The next two years seemed to take forever as I walked to the library a few times each month looking for each new book as it came out; *The Belgariad* sparked my love of fantasy novels and led me retroactively to more famous works from J.R.R. Tolkien and many others. Science Fiction was my next favorite, starting with Heinlein's *Starship Troopers*. William Gibson's *Neuromancer* took me deeper into the idea of speculative fiction.

Several years ago, I went searching for novels written in Arabic that fell in the genres I loved most. That was when I first found Yasser Bahjatt's TED talk, leading me to the Yatakhayaloon group; it was clear that our compasses pointed in the same direction. I enjoyed reading HWJN in both languages and decided I would like to shift my translation focus from the workaday world towards the translation of speculative and science fiction and fantasy.

I first found the Arabic version of *Warriors and Warlocks* while I was studying for my MA in translation, where I was focused on literary translation. I followed Dr. Monther Alkabbani on Twitter, and we exchanged a few words about the possibility of me taking on this translation, but I with a full course load, a full-time job, and a family; the time was not right. It was only a few months after graduating that both Yasser and Monther reached out to talk about this translation, and I jumped at the chance.

The story covers some very interesting ground, from science and history to personal relations and the individual in society. At once familiar and strange, the style of storytelling is different from what we are used to in English. I took cues from many of my current favorite authors regarding worldbuilding; I used a little explanatory translation here and there where necessary, but I put my faith in you, the reader, to work out some of the cultural queues; our author does well in dealing with the unsaid through his wonderful worldbuilding.

This is my first full novel as a translator, and I found the experience exciting and surprising. One of the amazing things that happened to me came as I approached the end of my first draft. I had not read the novel before starting the translation, so the story unfolded very slowly for me as I worked. It was only as I approached the end that there was enough built up enough in my head to have the novel take shape as a story rather than just another phrase, sentence, or paragraph to translate. When I could see the shape of the whole, I could appreciate it even more. I am sure I will have that sense again when I finish reading the full trilogy.

Any translator will tell you a translation is never really complete; I can revisit something I translated more than a decade ago and curse my younger self for such blatantly poor work. I could certainly go back through another detailed editing pass with this novel and make even more changes, but there comes a time to let go. It would not be in the shape it is without the insightful reading and feedback of Dr. Monther and my beta readers, in particular Jasmine Isaacson and Janet Humphreys. After hours of translating and typing, one's eyes become blind to certain things, or the brain skips over them; I deeply appreciate their close reading and the red pens they brought to the table.

I hope you enjoy it as much as I did, and I hope this leads to more of Monther Alkabbani's books coming into English in the near future – along with others from Yatakhayaloon and speculative and science fiction and fantasy from rest of the Arabic-speaking world!

Tim Gregory

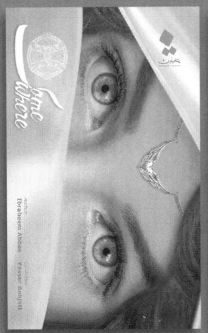

Author:
Ibraheem Abbas

Co-Author:
Yasser Bahjatt

English

H

W

J

N

Author:
Ibraheem Abbas

Co-Author:
Yasser Bahjatt

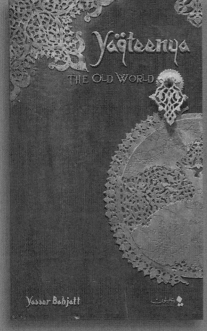

Yäqteenya

THE OLD WORLD

Yasser Bahjatt

BINYAMEEN

A BOOK BY
IBRAHEEM ABBAS
YASSER BAHJATT